THE WITCHING HOURS

BOOK ONE

BOOKS IN
THE WITCHING HOURS SERIES

THE VAMPIRE KNIFE

THE TROLL HEART
Available 2019

THE VAMPIRE KNIFE

JACK HENSELEIT

ART BY RYAN ANDREWS

Ⓣ Ⓡ

LITTLE, BROWN AND COMPANY

New York Boston

Text copyright © 2017 by Jack Henseleit
Illustrations copyright © 2017 by Ryan Andrews
Design copyright © 2017 by Hardie Grant Egmont
Cover art copyright © 2017 by Ryan Andrews

Little, Brown and Company
Hachette Book Group
1290 Avenue of the Americas, New York, NY 10104
Visit us at LBYR.com

Originally published in 2017 by Hardie Grant Egmont in Australia
First U.S. Edition: September 2018

Little, Brown and Company is a division of Hachette Book Group, Inc. The Little, Brown name and logo are trademarks of Hachette Book Group, Inc.

The publisher is not responsible for websites (or their content) that are not owned by the publisher.

Library of Congress Control Number: 2018936164

ISBNs: 978-0-316-52466-7 (hardcover), 978-0-316-52468-1 (ebook)

Printed in the United States of America

LSC-C

10 9 8 7 6 5 4 3 2 1

For Gypsy, Jesse, and Raffy—*the spookiest children*
in all of Mt. Rowan

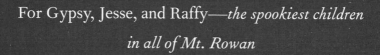

A WORD OF WARNING

The fairy tales recorded here do not take place
in the world we know. These are the stories of forests
dark and deep: legends from an old wood, where strange
and terrible creatures tread beneath the trees. These are
the stories of fairies in all their wild forms, their
bodies bloated with magic and with blood.

It would not be wise to meet these creatures.
It is, in any case, impossible. Their world is not our
world. Their paths are not our paths. Harboring
any desire to find them will lead only to
disappointment and despair.

Do not look for fairies.
You will not find them.

And if you do, you will regret it.

1

ALMOST THERE

WILL YOU TELL ME A STORY?" ASKED MAX.

Anna turned her head to try to look at him. The Professor had built a barricade of pillows and suitcases in the middle of the back seat to stop her and Max from kicking each other, and it had grown so high that all she could see now were the tips of his tufty brown hair. The rest of his face was hidden behind a pile of the Professor's textbooks.

"How about a game of I-spy?" said Max. "You can go first."

Anna glanced out the window. She sighed.

"There's just one problem, Max," she said. "I can't see anything."

It was a dark and stormy afternoon in Transylvania. Rain thundered down the hillside, drumming against the roof of the car as it twisted and turned along the mountain path. The car's headlights were struggling against the gloom.

Anna suspected they might be lost. It had been a long time since she had seen any road signs, and the current path was so narrow and rocky that it might not have been a road at all. The storm had made the first hour of the drive exciting. Now, at the end of the third hour, Anna was becoming concerned.

"Are we almost there?" she asked.

She pulled against her seatbelt so she could look into the front of the car. The Professor was gripping the wheel with both hands, his nose almost touching the windshield as he tried to see the road ahead. Every now and again he would look quickly at the passenger seat, which was piled high with charts and atlases. On the very top was the oldest map that Anna had ever seen. The paper was so worn and torn that it was beginning to break into pieces.

Anna cleared her throat.

"Are we almost there?" she asked in a loud voice.

The Professor jumped, and the car wobbled from one side of the road to the other (which was not really very far at all).

"Yes, almost there," he said, looking nervously at the old map. He wiped his forehead. "At least, I think we are."

Anna groaned. It wouldn't be the first time the Professor had gotten them lost. She sat back into her seat and crossed her arms.

"I still have some gummies," said Max.

"Liar."

"I'm not a liar. I saved almost half of them."

"Show me."

Anna watched as a brown paper bag appeared above the barricade. It looked half full. Anna was impressed. She had finished all of her own candy more than two hours ago.

"I'll share them," said Max. "But you have to tell me a story."

A fork of lightning crashed into the nearby forest. Thunder boomed overhead so loudly that it might have been a giant ripping apart the sky.

"Deal," said Anna.

A red gummy snake sailed over the pile of suitcases and landed in her lap.

"Don't make it too scary," said Max. "Just a little scary."

Anna picked up the snake and bit its head off.

"All right," she said. "Give me a minute to think."

Anna chewed up the rest of the snake, staring out the window at the dark woods. She smiled to herself.

And then the story began.

"Once upon a time," said Anna, "there was a little boy named Max, who was only eight years old. Max lived in the city with his sister, who was eleven, and their father, who was called the Professor. One day the Professor took Max and his sister on a work trip, to a great forest that was growing in the middle of nowhere. But Max should never have entered the forest."

"Why not?"

"Because in the forest it was always night, and it was always raining, and the paths were so long and overgrown that even the Professor could get lost. But even worse were the things that lived beneath the trees. And worst of all, in the deepest, darkest center of the woods…" Anna paused for dramatic effect. "There was a witch."

"I want to stop the story for a minute," said Max quickly.

Anna stopped. She was glad Max couldn't see how widely she was smiling.

"First of all," said Max, "I want you to know that I'm not scared of witches anymore. So I don't mind that there's a witch in the story. Okay?"

"Okay," said Anna.

"But I said to make it only a little scary. So I don't want anything bad to happen to Max, all right?"

"You always say that," said Anna. "But you know that *something* has to happen to him."

"Anna, be nice," called the Professor from the front seat. "Why don't you read to Max from your book instead?"

Anna wrinkled her nose. The Professor had

bought her a fairy book at the airport, but it was the wrong kind. The cover was bright and glittery pink, and the fairies in the story weren't even a little scary. The books she liked (sealed in her suitcase, buried somewhere in the great pile) were *real* fairy stories—the kinds with witches and goblins who played dangerous tricks on unwary girls and boys. The children would usually have to win their freedom from the enchanted forest, outsmarting the fairies. Sometimes they would even take some magical treasure back with them.

But the stories didn't always have happy endings. Sometimes the monsters won.

Anna shivered.

"No thanks," she said. She kicked the pink fairy book farther under the passenger seat. "We've already started this one."

"Yes, we have," said Max. "And it's okay, because Max is going to be fine, isn't he?"

Anna didn't answer the question. She continued the story instead.

"Max knew that he wasn't supposed to go into the forest. But after a while he began to feel a little braver, and he started to play closer and closer to the trees. Then one day, Max felt *even braver*, braver than he had ever felt before. He thought that going into the woods might be a good adventure.

"And he decided to take a step in."

There was a flash of lightning, and even Anna jumped. For a second she could see the forest outside, lit up as if it were a sunny day. The trees were old and warped, with curved branches that stretched out toward the road like wooden arms. Some of the twigs looked like fingers, long and sharp.

"What was that?" said Max. He sounded terrified.

"It was just lightning," said Anna.

"Not that. I saw something. In the woods."

"What? What was it?"

Anna craned her neck to look out Max's window, but the lightning had passed. All she could see was blackness.

"I don't know," said Max. "It looked like a person. A tall person, with white eyes."

"It was probably just a bear," said the Professor. "Transylvania is full of bears. Wolves too."

Anna thought that seeing a bear would have been pretty cool.

"It wasn't a bear," said Max. "It was something else. It was looking right at me."

"Well, I think it was a bear," said the Professor. "And I think we've heard enough of your story for now, Anna."

"Fine," said Anna. She crossed her arms. "I think we've had enough of your map reading," she added quietly.

The storm was getting worse. The rain was beating down harder than ever, rumbling loudly against the top of the car. Anna hoped the roof wouldn't collapse. Nobody said anything as they drove deeper into the forest.

Then another gummy snake dropped onto her lap.

Anna grinned. She turned toward the barricade and quietly started pulling away at the bags and books, dropping each one down at her feet. A few seconds later, she heard Max start to burrow from the other side. The barricade wobbled precariously— but then the final bag slid away and the tunnel was complete, and there was Max, looking in from the other side of the hole. Anna had the peculiar feeling that she was peering at someone through a library shelf.

"Finish the story!" whispered Max.

Anna shot a sneaky glance toward the Professor.

"Okay," she said. "Here's what happened next.

"Max knew that the forest paths could not be

trusted and that he would have to find his own way home. He had some bread in his pocket, and he crumbled it up and left a trail behind him."

"That's from *Hansel and Gretel*," said Max.

"He knew that he would be able to follow the breadcrumbs when he wanted to turn back and that they would lead him safely out through the trees."

"No they won't," said Max. "The birds will eat them."

Anna glared at him.

"Max thought that the birds might eat the breadcrumbs," she said. "But they didn't. It was an evil forest, and all of the birds and small animals had been scared away a long time ago. All that remained were the bears and the wolves—and the witch.

"And Max didn't know this, but it would have been a lot safer if the birds *had* eaten the breadcrumbs, because the trail he had made could be followed in two directions. If you went one way, the trail would lead a person out of the forest. But if the trail was followed the *other* way, it would lead a person *straight to Max*."

The car slowed to a stop. Anna sat up, worried that the story might have been overheard, but the Professor was distracted. His face was pressed up against the window, squinting hopefully.

"This might be the place," he said. "I'll have to get out and check. Will you be okay on your own for a moment?"

"Yes," said Anna.

"Yes," said Max, less confidently.

The Professor smiled at them reassuringly. He opened the car door, and for a second the wind outside could be heard at full volume, whispering and whistling and churning and roaring in great, rainy gusts. Then the door slammed shut, and the storm was muted once more.

The two children suddenly felt very alone.

"Don't tell any more of the story until Dad gets back," said Max.

"Are you sure?" said Anna. "The next part's really good."

"Is it scary?"

"It's a little bit scary."

Max couldn't help himself. "All right. Keep going."

Anna smiled.

"So Max crept quietly through the forest, leaving the trail of breadcrumbs behind him. But what he didn't realize was that someone was creeping along behind him. He didn't know that someone was getting closer and closer—almost close enough to touch him."

Max's face went very still. Anna leaned forward so her face filled the tunnel, smiling so that her teeth were showing. She made her voice go low and spooky.

"It was very dark beneath the trees, so dark that Max could barely see a thing. But the person was so close now that Max heard a footstep that was not his own. And he finally realized that someone—or something—was lurking in the blackness.

"And so Max looked back."

The real Max, who couldn't help himself, glanced quickly over his shoulder at the window behind him.

And at that moment, his car door was thrown open.

The storm rushed into the car. Anna was blinded as the rain gusted into her face; she rubbed her eyes, confused, trying to figure out what was going on. She could hear Max screaming, but she didn't know why—was it just the surprise of the door opening, or had something else happened? Anna swiftly undid her seatbelt and pushed herself up so she could see over the barricade.

The storm rushed into the car.

What she saw made her gasp in fright.

A wrinkled old woman was reaching into the car, her withered hands stretching out from beneath a long, black cloak.

She was reaching straight for Max.

2

THE WILD THYME INN

MAX YELLED AND SHOUTED AS THE OLD woman's hands undid his seatbelt and pulled him out of the car. Anna was speechless, her mouth hanging open. Then the door on Anna's side opened too, and suddenly someone was grabbing her around the waist and trying to pick her up. Anna spun around, her fingernails raised like claws, ready to confront whatever monster was attacking her.

It was the Professor.

"Calm down!" he said. "We need to get out of this storm!"

"But…but…" Anna was having difficulty speaking. "There's a witch! A witch took Max!"

"What?" said the Professor. "No, there aren't any witches. That was the innkeeper. Come on, let's go!"

Anna allowed the Professor to scoop her out of the car and half-tuck her under his raincoat. Then they were running through the storm, and big, cold raindrops were splashing against the top of Anna's head. Where were they going? It was only the middle of the afternoon, but Anna couldn't see anything through the fog. She narrowed her eyes, concentrating hard, and finally saw two faint squares of yellow light that must have been windows. She ducked out from under the raincoat and ran toward them as fast as she could.

Max was there already, struggling to free himself from the old woman's clutches. He saw Anna and shouted in desperation.

"Anna! Help me!"

"It's okay, Max! She's not a witch!" Anna called back. "I hope," she added under her breath.

The inn was emerging unwillingly from the darkness. The building looked like it belonged in a different century. The white stone walls were overgrown with vines and moss, and the wood on the front door was warped and scarred. Rain was flowing off the edges of the thatched roof like a thousand tiny waterfalls.

There was also a sign by the door, propped up by a pot filled with small purple flowers. The painted letters were chipped and faded, but Anna could still read what they said: THE WILD THYME INN.

"*Alo*," said the old woman. She smiled down at Anna.

Anna wondered what *alo* meant. "Alo? Oh—hello."

The old woman nodded and smiled again. She didn't have very many teeth. Max was now standing very still, his eyes screwed shut. He kept them closed until the Professor arrived on the tiny veranda, shivering and shaking the rain out of his hair.

"What a downpour!" he said. "I doubt they'll let me into the library if I can't find a way to dry off."

The children immediately deflated.

"You don't have to go to the library right away, do you?" asked Max timidly.

Anna hoped he wouldn't leave either. Children were never allowed in the old libraries where the Professor did his research, and once he started reading they never knew when he might come back. This was usually okay, because Anna and Max knew they were allowed to watch as many movies as they wanted to until the Professor came back, and they could even have candy for dinner if he got back late enough. But this time, things were different. Even if the inn had a television (which Anna doubted), it wasn't the kind of place where the children wanted to be left alone.

"I can stay for lunch," said the Professor. He grinned at them, but Anna could tell he was just trying to cheer them up. "And after that, you'll get to play games with your babysitter." He gestured to the old woman. "Anna and Max, meet Mrs. Dalca."

The woman gave them another relatively toothless smile.

"*Prânz?*" she said in a croaky voice. Seeing that they didn't understand, she tried again, searching for the English word. "Lunch?" Her accent was very thick.

21

"Yes, please," said the Professor. "We're really hungry."

Anna was surprised to find that she really did feel like a hot meal; she'd been too distracted to realize just how cold it was. She followed the woman—*Mrs. Dalca*, she remembered—and the Professor into the inn. Max walked very closely next to Anna, glad to be free of the old lady's clutches. He was still shivering.

The inn was warmer inside, but not by much. A fire burned at the base of a thick stone chimney, tickling the bottom of a brass cooking pot that hung above the flames. All of the furniture was made of twisted wood, and most of it looked dusty from disuse. Anna suspected they were the first guests to stay at the inn for a while.

"Look at that," whispered Max. He pointed at the cooking pot. "That looks like a cauldron."

"No it doesn't," said Anna. It did look a little

like a cauldron, but for now Anna wasn't interested in scaring Max. She was too close to feeling scared herself.

The Professor sat them down at a long table in the center of the room. Mrs. Dalca shuffled over to the fire, lifting the lid off the pot and sniffing whatever was inside. Anna wrinkled her nose. She could smell the contents of the pot all the way from where she was sitting, and it didn't smell good. It was like a strange mixture of onion and cloves, along with some other things she couldn't identify.

Most of all, it smelled like garlic.

Max had smelled it too. He was sniffing the air like a dog, scrunching up his nose.

"That smells disgusting," he said.

The Professor gave Max a stern look. "That's a very rude thing to say."

Anna thought that it probably was very rude, but it was also very true.

Mrs. Dalca took the pot off the fire and dished out three bowls of the soupy stew. She carried them over to the table one at a time, beaming.

"Isabella! *Linguri!*" she called over her shoulder.

A girl appeared from a room behind the kitchen, carrying a selection of spoons. Anna guessed the girl must be a similar age to herself. She had long, dark, curly hair, and was wearing a neat white dress decorated with squiggly red patterns. Anna noticed there was a scar on the girl's cheek, shaped like a tiny crescent moon.

"Hello," said the Professor. "You must be Isabella."

The girl nodded. She smiled politely as she delivered them each a spoon.

Anna tried to give the girl her nicest smile. If she and Max had someone their own age to play with, then their stay in the inn might not be so bad after all.

"*Alo*," Anna said carefully. She hoped that she said it right.

The girl looked at her shyly. "*Alo*," she said. Then she ran back through the kitchen and disappeared.

Mrs. Dalca was still watching them.

"*Poftă bună!*" she said in her crackly voice. Anna could tell from the way she said it that she meant *dig in!*

The soup-stew was a murky green color, and the bowls were steaming ferociously. The Professor scooped up a spoonful and blew on it carefully before slipping it into his mouth.

"Delicious!" he proclaimed.

According to the Professor, most things were delicious, including every type of vegetable. Max stirred his own bowl doubtfully, his nose still wrinkled.

"I think it might be poisonous," he said.

"Don't be silly," said the Professor. "Eat up."

Anna bravely picked up her spoon. She hoped the other girl might try to warn her if the meal was dangerous, but she could see no sign of her. She dipped the spoon into the soup and took a very small sip.

The soup was not delicious, but it didn't taste poisonous either. The flavors were strong, like all the things Anna had smelled in the air: herby tastes that fizzed across her tongue and burned the back of her throat. She choked a little bit as she swallowed, surprised by the pepperiness.

Max's eyes widened. "It *is* poisonous," he said.

"No," spluttered Anna. "It's just hot."

But Max could not be convinced. When the Professor left the table to bring in their bags, Max quickly carried his bowl over to one of the purple-flower potted plants. The liquid bubbled sluggishly as he poured it all away.

"All done!" he said with a grin.

Anna rolled her eyes.

After the lunch dishes had been cleared away, Mrs. Dalca showed them to their rooms. Anna and Max were sharing a bedroom at the very back of the inn, with two small beds and a rickety old wardrobe. A startled mouse ran into a hole as they walked in.

"Oh, great," said Anna sarcastically.

The Professor put their suitcases on the floor and walked over to the window. Behind the inn stood a shed that might have been a henhouse; beyond that there was a small, grassy field, which separated the inn from the forest. The window pane was streaked with water. It didn't look like the weather was improving.

"You'll have a great view of the mountains once the rain clears," he said. "The Romanian countryside is supposed to be beautiful."

"Does it always rain like this?" asked Anna.

"I'm not sure. Maybe you could ask Mrs. Dalca."

The Professor knelt down so he could look the children in the eye. "I'm going to have to leave now. Can I trust you to behave?"

"Yes," said Anna.

"Yes," said Max.

"Good," said the Professor. He hugged them together firmly. "And if she is a witch," he whispered, "just push her into the oven."

The children giggled.

3

HIDDEN THINGS

THE CHILDREN WAVED AT THE PROFESSOR as he drove away, the car vanishing almost immediately into the shadows of the forest. Back in their room, Anna unpacked her suitcase. She had brought three books of fairy tales on the trip, and she stood them all up on the bedside table between two candlesticks. The covers were battered after years of being constantly read and re-read, but their presence seemed to brighten up the room.

"There could be secret passages in an old hotel like this," said Max.

Max's unpacking had consisted of finding his stash of emergency candy. He popped one in his mouth and looked around the bedroom.

"Let's look in the wardrobe. Sometimes they have magical worlds in them," he said.

Anna knew there probably weren't any magical worlds inside the wardrobe, but she thought exploring it might be a fun way to pass the time. She and Max walked to the wardrobe together. Max grabbed the handle.

"Ready?" he asked.

"Ready."

Max threw open the door. A whirlwind of dust rushed into their faces, causing both children to cough and splutter. And then:

"Nothing," said Max, disappointed. The wardrobe was empty.

"Hang on," said Anna. She took a step back and stood on her tiptoes, stretching her neck as far as it would go. "I think there's something on top of the wardrobe."

Max climbed onto his bed. He jumped up and down on the mattress, trying to get a better look.

"There *is* something," he said. "If you lift me up, then I might be able to grab it."

"Okay," said Anna. Max jumped off the bed. Anna grabbed him under the arms and lifted him above her head, trying to hold him steady as he poked his hands over the top of the wardrobe.

"Got it!" said Max.

Anna dropped her brother down. Whatever he was holding on to slid after him, getting bigger and bigger as it unraveled from its hiding place. Suddenly it was enormous, falling over them in a cloud of dust and darkness. It blocked the light completely.

"Get it off me!" yelled Max.

Anna was still choking on dust. She grabbed a fistful of the mystery object and tugged it away from her body. She could tell by touching it that it was made of fabric.

Max scrambled along the floor to escape. Once free, he turned to look at what Anna was holding.

"Oh," he said. "It's just a blanket."

Anna examined the thing in her hand. It did look like a blanket, but it also seemed slightly too long and slightly too narrow. The colors were wrong too. The blankets on their beds were brown and drab. This material was a rich, deep blue, with an area in the middle that was almost golden.

"I think it might be something else," she said. "Help me straighten it out."

The children spread the not-blanket across the floor, straightening the fabric until it was smooth. They stood up to admire their work, puzzling over the long, thin rectangle.

"It's a banner," said Anna at last. "Like the kind they hang in a castle."

Anna and Max stared at the banner together. It looked old—a lot older than anything else they had seen in the inn so far. At its center was a golden eagle, its wings spread majestically on either side of its body. The bird's talons were wrapped around a crescent moon, as if the eagle was trying to steal it from the evening sky.

"Do you think this is treasure?" asked Max.

"I...don't know," said Anna. She hadn't been expecting to find anything like this. "I guess it might be treasure to the person who hid it."

"Let's look for more things," said Max. He

lowered himself to the ground and rolled along the floor. A second later he had disappeared beneath Anna's bed.

But Anna hadn't finished looking at the banner. She stared curiously at the eagle's yellow eye, which was wicked and curved. She half expected it to blink at her.

"Hey, Anna!" called Max excitedly. "There's something under here!"

Anna was about to ask what it was when she heard footsteps in the corridor outside. Without thinking, she grabbed the banner and bundled it into her arms. She didn't know why, but for some reason she didn't want to be caught looking at it.

"Someone's coming," she hissed to Max. "Get out of there, quick!"

There was a noise from under the bed that sounded as if Max had bumped his head. Anna spun around to the wardrobe and stuffed the banner inside. She had just turned back around when the bedroom door swung open with a loud bang.

Mrs. Dalca stood in the doorway. Her eyes were narrowed.

"Come with me," she said.

Anna wasn't ready to leave their discoveries behind. "We'd like to stay here, please," she said in her politest voice.

Mrs. Dalca shook her head. "Too cold," she croaked. "Come to the fire."

She said it firmly, the way that teachers spoke when they were not in the mood to be argued with. Anna saw that they didn't have any choice. The old woman led them into the corridor, shutting the bedroom door firmly behind them. Anna realized too late that she had forgotten to grab one of her books.

They returned to the main room of the inn. The view through the windows was so misty and dark that it was beginning to feel like the middle of the night. Anna had to admit that it felt good to be closer to the fire.

Mrs. Dalca took a seat in the corner of the room and picked up a bundle of knitting. She began to weave with her hands, looping the wool around until it looked like her fingers were tied up with knots. Anna had never seen someone knit without needles. She wasn't sure what the old woman was making, but the wool was pure black, and Anna couldn't shake the feeling that this might be how witches made their clothes.

"Isabella!" called the old woman suddenly. "*Joc!*"

The girl with the scar on her cheek appeared again from a side room. She bravely walked up to the siblings and gave them a friendly smile.

"*Alo*," she said. "My name is Isabella."

"Hi," said Anna. She was surprised that the girl spoke English so well. "My name is Anna, and this is Max."

Max gave Isabella a tentative wave. Anna found herself staring at the mark on the girl's cheek. It was shiny and white, just like how the real moon looked on a clear evening.

"I like your scar," she said.

"Thanks," said Isabella. "I got it from falling out of a tree. I was trying to get all the way to the top, but one of the branches snapped, and I got scratched on the way down." She ran a finger over her cheek, suddenly shy. "I like it, though. It's like a present from the forest."

Anna took off her shoe to expose one of her own scars: a long, snaky line that curved along the side of her foot.

"I got this one in a lake," she said. "A branch had fallen in, and I kicked it while I was swimming over the top of it."

"That's a good one," said Isabella. She giggled. "Maybe it was a friend of the branch that got me."

Anna laughed too. She decided that she liked Isabella.

"Do you want to play a game?" asked Isabella. "Granny Dalca won't mind, as long as she sees us all near the fire every couple of minutes."

"Yes, please," said Anna. She hadn't realized Mrs. Dalca was the girl's grandmother. "What do you want to play?"

"My favorite is hide-and-seek," said Isabella. "But I know all the best places now, so it might be unfair."

"I'm really good at hide-and-seek," piped up Max. "I bet I can find you."

Isabella grinned. "Okay. You count to thirty, and Anna and I will hide. Whoever gets found first has to help find the other one."

"Got it." Max covered his eyes. "One!" he said. "Two!"

The girls fled. Anna saw that the inn was full of good hiding places. There were cupboards for blankets in the hallway that a child could wriggle into, along with large wardrobes in most of the bedrooms. Isabella darted away before Anna could see where she was going; Anna found herself in front of a door at the very end of a hall.

"Thirty!" announced Max.

Anna grabbed the handle. It was a heavy door, with hinges that groaned. With a strong push she opened the door wide enough for a small girl to pass through. She slipped into the room.

Her eyes struggled to adapt to the gloomy half-light. It seemed that the room was being used for storage. The floor was covered with cardboard boxes and wooden crates, and a row of old cabinets lined one of the walls. Anna picked her way toward the largest cabinet and climbed inside, happy she found a hiding place.

She sat down and closed the door, and everything went black.

There was a large keyhole in the cabinet door. Anna placed her eye gently against the gap, trying not to make any noise. Max would sometimes peek during hide-and-seek when he was supposed to have his eyes closed. Had he seen which way she ran?

A whole minute went by. Anna looked glumly at the window on the opposite side of the room. It might have been a trick of the light, but it looked like the rain was coming down less fiercely against the glass, although it was still beating loudly on the roof. For a while, Anna listened to the rain, trying to enjoy its rhythm.

Then she heard the sound of groaning hinges.

Anna took a deep breath and held it, determined not to make a sound. She couldn't see the main door through the keyhole, but she was sure that someone was standing in the doorway, listening. She fixed her eye on the window, as still as a statue.

And so, when a flash of lightning tore through the sky only a second later, Anna saw something she was not meant to see. She saw the tall figure standing outside the window, its mouth wide open, its white eyes burning like fire.

And then the cabinet door swung open.

4

FORBIDDEN WORDS

FOUND YOU!" SAID MAX. HE BEAMED DOWN at Anna proudly.

Anna felt like her blood had turned to ice. She pointed at the window, her finger shaking.

"Did you see that?"

Max glanced at the window. "It was just lightning," he said.

Anna had a sudden sense of déjà vu. Hadn't they had this conversation already?

"That thing you saw in the forest," she said slowly. "The thing the Professor said was a bear. What did it look like?"

Max shrugged. "It was like a person," he said. "Except their eyes were white. A bright, shining white."

Anna knew exactly what he meant. She'd looked into those eyes.

They'd been staring right at her.

"Something's wrong with this place," she said. She climbed out of the cabinet, holding on to Max's arm. "We need to get out of here. We need to find the Professor, and then we need to leave."

Max frowned. "It's not that bad here. Dad will be back soon."

Anna grabbed Max's shoulders. "I saw it. I saw

that thing you saw. It was standing right there, looking in. It was watching us."

Max turned to face the window. The forest was dark again, and the rain was still pattering against the glass. Whatever had been there was gone now.

"Maybe it *was* just a bear," he said.

"It wasn't a bear," said Anna. "You were right. It was…" She stopped to think. If it wasn't a bear, what was it? It had been very tall and very thin, with a face so pale that it was almost like a phantom. It hadn't looked entirely human, but it also hadn't looked like any animal Anna had seen before. There was only one thing she was sure of: *it* was not their friend.

"It doesn't matter what it was," she said. "We need to get out of here." She squeezed Max's shoulders. His face was scrunched up tightly, a sign that he was thinking hard. Anna sighed. Ever since Max had turned eight he'd stopped listening to her as much as he used to, and the two of them had been fighting more than ever before. Why couldn't he realize how important this was?

"Okay." Max nodded. "Let's call Dad."

Anna hugged him in relief.

The children held hands as they walked out into the hallway, almost breaking into a run as they approached the main room. Mrs. Dalca was still knitting in the corner, weaving her fingers nimbly through the ever-growing tangle of black yarn. It looked like she was holding a living shadow.

"Excuse me," said Anna. "Is there a telephone we can use?"

Mrs. Dalca looked up at them. Her fingers kept moving.

"*Nu*," she said. "There is no phone."

"Oh." Anna's voice faltered a little. "We would like to see the Professor. Can you take us to him?"

Mrs. Dalca shook her head.

"It will soon be night," she said. "We will stay here."

Anna looked closely at Mrs. Dalca. Something had changed in the old woman's face when she had said the word *night*. It wasn't a look that Anna liked.

There was a coughing noise behind them, and the children jumped. They turned and saw that Isabella had walked into the room.

"Did you give up?" she asked. "I told you I'm good at hiding."

Anna didn't know what to say. Max was standing stiffly beside her, his face scrunched up again. Anna could guess what he was thinking: if Mrs. Dalca wanted to keep them trapped inside the inn, then there might be a chance that Isabella—her granddaughter—was helping her with the plan. Could the girl be trusted? They had no way of knowing.

"Isabella!" interrupted Mrs. Dalca. *"Avem nevoie de lemn. Focul se stinge."*

Anna wished that she understood Romanian. Isabella listened closely, and when the old woman finished speaking she nodded in agreement.

"Would you like to come outside with me?" she asked. "I'm just going to the back of the house, to the woodpile."

"No thanks," blurted Anna. She looked down at Max, desperately trying to think of an excuse. "Max is getting a cold," she lied. "We'd better stay inside so it doesn't get any worse."

Max sniffed helpfully.

"Adu usturoi," croaked Mrs. Dalca.

"Oh. All right then," said Isabella to Anna. "I'll see you in a minute."

The siblings watched in silence as the girl pulled on a pair of rainboots and wrapped a thick black scarf around her neck. She opened the inn door without looking back at them, and a moment later she was gone. She seemed a little sad, making Anna feel guilty.

"What do we do now?" whispered Max.

Anna was still staring at the door. "We could make a run for it," she said. "How far away do you think the library is?"

As if in reply, a huge flash of lightning surged across the sky. It ran along the treetops like a ribbon, illuminating the countless drops of rain suspended in midair. The thunder followed immediately with a great explosion, bursting so loudly above them that the walls of the inn seemed to tremble.

"I don't think we should make a run for it," said Max.

Mrs. Dalca had put down her knitting and was muttering furiously to herself. She was holding one of her wrinkled hands in front of her face, twisting her fingers around like she was trying to weave the air itself.

"*Fantomă furtună*," she said. "*Strigoi furtună. Dispari!*"

Anna looked up, confused. One of the old woman's words had stuck in her head, half-remembered, almost forgotten. She tried to recall where she had heard it before, but the memory drifted away before she could catch it. She decided to throw caution to the wind.

"Mrs. Dalca? What does *strigoi* mean?" she asked.

The old woman's eyes opened wide.

"You must not use that word," she rasped. "I forbid it."

"Why not?" Anna was starting to feel frustrated with the woman's rules. "What will happen if I say *strigoi*? If I accidentally said *strigoi*, would that annoy you?"

Mrs. Dalca rose swiftly to her feet. Her face had become as dark as the raging storm.

"Stop it now, or I will lock you in the cupboard!" she spluttered.

Anna decided they'd better run for it. As one, the siblings fled down the hallway; they skidded into their bedroom together, slamming the door closed. Anna saw with dismay that it couldn't be locked.

"What now?" asked Max, panting.

They could hear Mrs. Dalca cursing from the main room. Anna pushed all of her weight against the door, afraid that the woman would try to open it, but nobody came. Eventually she slid down to the floorboards, sitting cross-legged with her head in her hands.

"She doesn't have to come and get us," she said miserably. "We're still trapped inside the inn. She can do whatever she wants to us."

She looked up at Max, waiting for him to cry. Max was the youngest, and so was always the first one to get upset. As soon as she saw him shed a tear, she would be allowed to cry too.

But Max surprised her. He sat next to her and held her hand, squeezing it tightly with his small fingers.

"Something mysterious is happening," he said. "And we're the only ones who can solve it. We need to put all the pieces together and figure out what's going on. You're good at this stuff, Anna. It's like one of your fairy tales. We need to outsmart the bad guys."

It's like one of your fairy tales.

Anna gasped. Max was right—and two of the pieces were already coming together in her mind.

"I know where I've seen that word before!" she said.

She jumped to her feet and walked across the room. Her books were waiting patiently for her on the bedside table. She picked up the smallest one, an old, thin book with a faded red cover. The gold lettering on the front had almost flaked away entirely, but the title could still be read: *Fairy Tales for Daring Children*. It was the oldest book she owned, and the book she had owned the longest. The Professor said that she must have taken it from his study when she was a baby, though Anna wasn't sure how this was possible; for all his absentmindedness, the Professor was always sure to keep his study locked up tight. Despite mentioning the story often, the Professor had never taken the book back—and so it had become one of Anna's greatest treasures.

She flicked through the pages. The stories in the first half of the book were wonderfully scary, but the second half was even better. It listed all the rules a child would need to follow if they ever entered an enchanted forest, including all the ways to overcome the various fairies and their spells. Anna knew most of the major rules by heart. *Do not accept food from a fairy. Do not tell a fairy your real name. If you are on a quest, do not tell a fairy where you are going or what you hope to do.* Anna skimmed past passages about trolls and genies, mermaids and dragons, until she finally found what she was looking for. She began to read aloud from a dog-eared page.

"'When a fairy dies, their magic does not always die with them. The trapped magic can sometimes transform their body into an entirely different creature: a monster that can only sustain itself by drinking the blood of the living. These undead fairies are known by many names, including *lilitu*, *mandurugo*, *jiangshi*, and *strigoi*.'"

She had found the word—but what did it mean? She quickly read ahead to the next sentence. A chill shivered down her spine.

"What else does it say?" said Max.

Anna swallowed nervously.

"'However, the blood-sucking creatures are most commonly known as *vampires*.'"

The bedroom door crashed open. Mrs. Dalca strode into the room, her eyes ablaze.

"You are very bad children," she said in a wheezing voice. "You will go to bed without any supper."

Anna thought that seemed like a great punishment; she didn't want to eat any more of Mrs. Dalca's soup-stew anyway. She hid the book of fairy tales behind her back, hoping that the old woman hadn't seen it.

"What is that?" said Mrs. Dalca. "What is in your hand?"

Anna was cornered. The woman bore down on her, prying the shabby red book from her fingers. Mrs. Dalca held it close to her face, mouthing the words of the title. Then she smiled.

"I will take this," she said triumphantly. "There will be no more stories tonight!"

5

THE WITCHING HOUR

ANNA HADN'T EXPECTED THE SKY TO GET any darker, but now the true night was falling upon the forest, and the mist was growing thicker with every new shadow. Strange noises began to echo through the woods, carried by the wind: the scratching sounds of something moving beneath the trees, often followed by the faintest trace of a howl.

The old witch had stolen their book. Anna wished she had read faster, or skipped ahead to the part about repelling the monsters—or, better yet, defeating them. She could only remember what every child her age knew: that vampires were allergic to sunlight, could sometimes turn into bats or other small animals, and could be driven away by certain plants. But how much of that was true, and how much of it had been invented by storytellers? When was the last time someone had actually encountered a *real* vampire? Anna hoped her old fairy book would have some answers.

Their plan was simple. They would wait until the middle of the night, when Mrs. Dalca was asleep. Then they would find the book and steal it back.

The only problem was that the children were exhausted.

To try to keep herself awake, Anna took the eagle banner back out of the wardrobe, carefully spreading it out on the floor. It was a piece of the puzzle she was determined to solve, though she wasn't sure how it fit yet. She ran her hands over the golden wings, brushing the dust from the tips of the feathers. She covered the bird's eye, stretching her fingers out to touch the wicked curve of its beak. Nothing helped. The banner seemed to be from a completely different puzzle.

"I'm getting tired," she said with a yawn.

Max was sitting on the bed. He checked the clock on the bedside table. It was only nine o'clock.

"Mrs. Dalca won't be asleep yet," he said. "We have to stay up later."

"We won't be able to sneak around if we're tired," said Anna. "We should have a nap."

Max frowned as he considered it. Anna's tiredness felt like a warm blanket across her shoulders. So many things had happened since they arrived in Transylvania. Didn't they deserve a rest?

"A nap is a good idea," said Max. "But we'll have to take it in turns, so someone can stay awake and be the lookout. I'll watch first if you want."

Anna smiled gratefully. She stood up and saw that Max was chewing away on his gummies, filling his body with sugary energy. No wonder he didn't feel as sleepy as she did.

"Wake me up at ten-thirty," she said. She slipped under the heavy brown cover, snuggling deep into the bed.

Max might have said something in reply, but the words were muddled by her drowsiness. In no time at all, Anna was fast asleep.

And soon she was dreaming.

The garden is beautiful. There are flowers of every shape and color, all dancing slowly in the gentle breeze. The garden is a happy place.

The garden has been built in the courtyard of a great castle. There are banners flying from the castle battlements. It is hard to see the banners clearly. Sometimes the banners look blue, but at other times they look red, or even yellow.

Sometimes they look like bats.

In the castle there is a secret panel. Beyond the panel is a staircase, which leads to a white stone passage. At the end of the passage is a dungeon. The dungeon has an iron door.

The dungeon was built to hold the creature. The creature has been sentenced to live in the dungeon until the end of time. The only rule of the castle is that the creature must never leave.

The iron door is open.

The white stone passage is cold and quiet. The doorway at the end of the passage is full of darkness, like a cavity in the side of a tooth.

It is time to run. It is time to run away from the dungeon, along the white stone passage, up the staircase, out through the secret panel. The garden will be waiting. The garden is a happy place.

The creature is very fast.

Max and the Professor are standing on the staircase. They call out along the white stone passage, beckoning with their hands.

"Run, Anna! Don't look back! Run as fast as you can!"

Running in the castle feels like walking. The staircase moves farther away with every step. The calls of encouragement grow fainter and fainter.

The creature has a wide mouth. Its teeth are narrow and sharp.

The teeth are dripping.

Drip.

Drip.

Drip.

Anna woke with a start. She felt like her body had just fallen onto the bed from a great height; her breathing was short and ragged. She stared up at the ceiling, which was not the ceiling of a white stone passage. It took her a few moments to realize she had been dreaming. She slowly remembered where she was sleeping, and why.

None of this explained why she could still feel something dripping onto her forehead.

Anna slowly turned to look across the dark room. The clock face stared back at her from the bedside table. A drop of water was running down its spindly hands, which were both pointed directly upward. It was midnight—she should have been woken hours ago. Max must have fallen asleep. All she could see of him was a clump of tufty hair emerging from under the blanket.

Worse still, the window had blown open. Rain

was spattering its way into the room, dripping icily onto her nose and cheeks. Her remaining books were strewn across the floor, knocked over by the wind. Anna pulled the blanket over her head. She felt too warm and comfortable to retrieve the books. Was it possible that nothing bad was going to happen to them after all? If Mrs. Dalca had an evil plan, then surely she would have carried it out while the children were sleeping.

Anna reasoned that if she went to sleep again now, it would probably be morning when she woke up. By then the Professor might have returned, and he would be able to make everything all right. They could drive away from the Wild Thyme Inn and never look back.

All she had to do was close the window.

The room was colder now. Anna wriggled out from beneath the blanket, scowling as the spray of the rain began to chill the soles of her feet. The floorboards creaked with every step. Much like Anna, they seemed unhappy about being disturbed so late at night.

The window shutters were flapping madly. Anna grabbed onto the left shutter and tried to wrestle it shut, pushing back against the bluster. In all her life, she had never encountered such a wild storm. Gusts of wind were swinging through the window like punches, crashing into her body so violently that she felt as if she might be knocked over. With a mighty shove she rammed the first shutter closed. Now the window looked like a butterfly with only one wing, fluttering frenziedly in the breeze. Anna quickly reached for the second shutter. Her fingers were almost completely numb.

And then she stopped. There was a sound coming from the forest that had not been there before, a sound that was being snatched from somewhere on the mountainside and carried through the window by the wicked wind. Strange noises nestled in Anna's ears. They felt like words, but they were being spoken so far away that she couldn't tell what the words were supposed to be.

Was there someone out there, lost in the woods?

Anna couldn't see anything. The moon was milky and pale, hanging in the heavens like a great blind eye. The storm clouds were devouring most of the starlight before it could reach the forest; the little light that did pierce through was instantly smothered by fog.

But still there was a calling—and it was a calling now, becoming slightly clearer with every new rush of wind. The voice was desperate, screaming even, shrieking its message across the night. Anna glanced at Max's tufty hair. Should she wake him? Would he be able to help?

She turned her head, concentrating hard, hoping to hear a clear word, a clear instruction. She ignored the sting of the rain on her cheek, searching only for the sound, focusing on the strange fragments of noise.

And then, a gust of wind finally carried a whole sentence into her ear.

"Anna! Look out!"

Anna gasped. She knew that voice. She had known it for eight entire years.

The clouds parted. A perfect moonbeam fell from the sky, illuminating the hillside with a blue-white glow. It landed on the back of a distant figure who was striding away from the inn, a bundle thrown over its shoulder like a sack. The bundle was shouting and beating its fists, bawling into the storm.

"Anna! Get out! It'll eat you!"

The figure holding the bundle turned around. It stared back at the inn with its eyes ablaze, shining out of the mist like a pair of distant stars.

The figure holding the bundle turned around.

It was then that Anna heard the growling.

There was something rising from beneath the blanket on Max's bed—something that was covered from head to toe in brown, tufty hair. Anna slowly backed away as the blanket fell loose, uncovering an animal she had hoped never to meet up close.

The bear growled. Its mouth curled back into a snarl, revealing four long, sharp teeth.

It stepped off the bed, claws raised, ready to attack.

6

UNDER THE BED

THE BEAR LASHED OUT WITH A PAW, swiping forward with a deadly punch. Anna threw herself onto the ground; the claws slashed the space where her head had been, raking viciously through the air. The bear's claws were like fingernails gone bad, hook-shaped and blackened. Anna knew they would have no problem tearing through a child.

The bear stood back on its hind legs and growled again. It was a horrible sound, somewhere between a dog's bark and a lion's roar, and it made every inch of Anna's skin prickle in pure terror. The bedroom door was too far away to escape through, so Anna crawled frantically underneath her bed and flattened herself against the far wall instead, her heart pounding so loudly that she was sure someone would hear it and come to her aid.

"Help!" she tried to call, her voice catching in her throat. "Somebody help me!"

The bear lowered its head to the floor and stared at her through small black eyes. Then it lunged, reaching out into the space beneath the bed, thrashing its arms. Anna watched as the claws sliced back and forth, inches from her face. She was too frightened to scream, so scared she could barely think. What could she do? How could a child defeat a fully grown bear? Anna churned furiously through all the possibilities.

Hey, Anna! There's something under here!

The memory rushed into Anna's mind. Max had thought he'd found something while she was busy examining the eagle banner—and he'd been under her bed when he'd said it.

The bear had retreated for a moment, rethinking its strategy. Anna ran her hands over the floor. Her fingertips left snail-lines as they dragged across the dusty floorboards, looping and curving in desperate arcs, probing at the shadows.

One of the floorboards wobbled.

A tiny bud of hope blossomed in Anna's chest. She dug her fingers underneath the wooden board and pried it upward. Two rusty iron nails hung from the bottom of the plank. They looked like the fangs of a certain monster that Anna was trying not to think about.

There was only one loose board. Anna stared at the small hole that had opened up in the floor, choking back her disappointment. A mouse might be able to escape through the tunnel, but certainly not an eleven-year-old girl.

The shaggy paws reappeared at the edge of the bed. The bedframe began to shake; the bear was standing again now, using its beastly strength to lift up Anna's hiding place.

Maybe there was a secret lever. Maybe it would activate a trapdoor, which would swing open and drop her to safety. Anna pushed her arm into the hole, blindly searching for the thing—anything—that would save her life.

Her fingers closed around a handle.

It felt like something had burst inside Anna's body. Adrenaline pumped through her arm as she pulled her hand out from the hollow, holding tightly on to the object that she was sure would save her.

The bed flipped over, crashing against the wall. The bear loomed above her, its teeth bared, arms raised in preparation for the final strike. Anna held out her hand, waving the mystery item between them.

"Stay back!" she said. "Go away!"

Neither of them moved. The bear stared at the thing in Anna's hand. Anna stared at it too.

She had no idea what it was.

The thing was about the length of a school ruler. It looked a bit like a sword, but no part of it was made of metal. The blade was thin and creamy-white, the same color as scar tissue, or the moon on a cloudy night. The edges looked very sharp, tapering to a point so fine and needlelike that Anna could scarcely see it in the unlit room.

The bottom of the knife (for Anna decided that it must be a knife) was wrapped in a leather coil. It felt warm and comfortable in her hand, almost like the knife had been sitting close to a fire. Holding on to it made her feel less afraid.

She watched the bear, waiting for it to move. The small black eyes were fixed on the dagger's point. They weren't blinking. For the first time, the creature looked uncertain, unsure of how to proceed.

And then the bear bowed. It sat down on its rump and leaned forward, placing its snout on the floor at Anna's feet. It made a small growling noise that sounded almost friendly.

All was quiet in the room. The tip of the knife wobbled in the air. Anna tried to stop her arm from trembling. For reasons she didn't understand, the fight was over. She reached out with her free hand and rubbed the bear between the ears. It purred a little louder, sniffing at her skin as she ran her fingers through its brown fur.

Anna decided it would be all right to cry. Tears slid down her face as she sat in the bedroom where Max had been stolen, patting the nose of the bear that had tried to devour her. She thought about the

Professor, away with his books, unaware that the children were in such terrible danger. She thought about home.

When she had finished crying she stood up. The bear looked at her inquiringly.

"You stay here," she said. "Or leave. I don't mind. But I'm leaving to go and rescue my brother."

She pointed the knife at Max's bed. The bear climbed atop the mattress and curled up with its head on its front paws. It gave her one final stare, then closed its eyes.

"Um. Good. Thank you," said Anna.

As she left the room, the bear began to snore.

Out in the hallway, Anna walked directly to Mrs. Dalca's room. The door was locked. Anna raised her fist and knocked on the door. She knocked again and again and again, tapping out a steady rhythm with her knuckles. Eventually she heard movement on the other side of the door, and then a voice spoke to her through the keyhole.

"*Ce vrei?*" It was Mrs. Dalca's voice, croakier than ever after being woken. "Who is that? What do you want?"

"It's Anna," said Anna. "I want my book back."

"Go away, wicked child," said the voice. "Go back to sleep."

"I can't sleep," said Anna. "There's a bear in my room, and I have to go and fight a vampire. So please give me my book. If you do, I'll stop knocking."

There was no reply. Anna thought she could hear muttering, but it was too soft to make out the words. She lifted her hand, ready to give the door a particularly loud knock.

Something moved in the shadows at the end of the hall. Anna spun around quickly, the knife held ready. The moving thing paused, hidden in the darkness. And then:

"Anna?" said a small voice. Isabella stepped into the hallway, still rubbing the sleep from her eyes. "What's wrong?"

Anna lowered the knife. She looked closely at the other girl. Could she be trusted?

"I want to see your grandmother," she said. "She took something from me, and now I need it back."

Isabella frowned. "Granny Dalca doesn't leave her room at night. She always keeps her door locked from dusk until dawn. She says it's safer that way."

"Isabella!" said the voice from the bedroom. "*Du-te înapoi la culcare!*"

"What did she say?" asked Anna.

"She says to go back to sleep. She doesn't like me walking around in the inn after bedtime." Isabella looked curiously at the knife in Anna's hand. "What's that?"

Anna gritted her teeth in frustration. "I need my book," she said. "Unless *you* can tell me how to defeat a vampire. Defeat a *strigoi*. Because one of them took Max, and I don't think I can wait much longer."

She said it as seriously as she could. To her surprise, Isabella just smiled.

"*Strigoi* aren't real," she said. "They're just a story that adults tell to scare children. Granny always says that if I don't eat my soup, the old count on the hill will come and carry me off. That's why she puts so much garlic into her soup—to keep the vampires away. But really it's because she likes the flavor."

Garlic—to keep the vampires away. It was as if the line had been taken right out of Anna's book of fairy tales. And with it came a memory: Max at lunchtime, grinning as he poured his soup onto the purple flowers.

"Max didn't eat any garlic," gasped Anna. "That's why the vampire could take him. We need to get him some soup!"

Isabella smiled again. "I think you might have had a bad dream," she said. "Let's go back to your room. I'm sure Max is fine."

"He isn't," said Anna.

But Isabella was already walking down the hallway to Anna's bedroom.

"Be careful," said Anna. "There's a bear in there."

Isabella opened the door. She stood perfectly still for five seconds, staring into the bedroom. Her face went very white. Then she leaned forward and shut the door.

"I changed my mind," she said. "I think we might be in very big trouble."

7

MYTHS AND MAPS

ISABELLA'S BEDROOM WAS BEHIND THE
kitchen. It was the closest room to the fireplace, and
so was much warmer than anywhere else in the inn.
The walls were covered in drawings of trees and
flowers, as if the forest had sneaked in through the
window and taken root.

Isabella walked over to her closet and pulled out
two rain jackets.

"Here," she said, passing one of the coats to Anna. "We'll definitely need these."

The rain jacket was black, and the inside was lined with soft fur. Anna thought it would be good camouflage in the darkness outside.

Isabella reached into the farthest corner of the closet and dragged out an old brown knapsack. The bottom of the bag was held together with several mismatched patches, and the shoulder straps were almost worn through. Isabella opened the top of the knapsack and pulled out a metal thermos.

"This is my adventure kit," she said. "I take it out with me when I go tree climbing. It's full of things that might help us."

There seemed to be an unspoken agreement that Isabella would help Anna find Max. Anna looked inside the knapsack. She could see a rope and a pocketknife and a rolled-up bandage, as well as a white paper sketchbook and a bundle of pencils. She found herself wishing that she had an adventure kit as good as this one.

"We could add your sword," said Isabella. "I could wrap it in a towel."

Isabella must have thought Anna had brought the knife with her to the inn. Anna decided to tell her the true story.

"It's not really mine," she said. "I found it in the bedroom, hidden underneath the floor." She placed the white knife on the edge of Isabella's bed. Her hand immediately felt colder.

Isabella looked at the blade curiously. She extended a finger toward it, gently touching the edge of the knife. She gasped. A cut had instantly appeared on her skin, deep enough that a drop of blood was already collecting on her fingertip. She quickly stuck her finger in her mouth to suck it away.

"I barely touched it!" she said.

Anna stared in amazement at the little dagger. "No wonder the bear was so afraid of me," she said. Isabella's room was well lit, but the tip of the knife remained difficult to see.

"It kind of looks like a tooth," said Isabella. "Do you think it has something to do with the vampire?"

"Yes," said Anna. "But I don't know what. Before we leave, I have a lot of questions to ask you."

Isabella nodded. "You want to know everything I can remember about the *strigoi*."

The two girls walked back into the kitchen, where the brass cooking pot was still hanging above the fire. Isabella emptied the water from the metal thermos into the sink. She picked up a ladle and began scooping the warm soup-stew into the thermos. The kitchen was soon filled with the smell of garlic.

"There is no village near our inn," began Isabella. "So there are very few people who live out here. Granny says they live in houses that are scattered through the woods, hidden from the rest of the world.

"But even though our community is very small, it still used to have a count. He lived high on the mountainside in his fortress, and it was his job to look after us and protect us."

Anna knew that a count was similar to a lord or lady. They were usually members of old families who had lived in the same place for hundreds of years, passing on the title from one generation to the next.

"But when Granny was young, the count died," continued Isabella. She screwed the cap back onto the thermos and pushed it into the adventure kit. "And he didn't have any children. And that's all true so far, I think. I always thought the next part was just a story."

She cast a dark look back toward Anna's bedroom. Anna knew what she was thinking. With Max missing and a bear sleeping in his place, even the strangest stories now sounded quite plausible. Isabella took a deep breath.

"The people in the area all came out of their houses in the woods and had a meeting," she said. "And someone said that the count had been cursed and that after he was buried he would come back and haunt everyone who lived in the forest. There was only one way to make sure he didn't become a *strigoi*."

"What? What was it?" asked Anna urgently.

Isabella picked up a log from the small woodpile and threw it onto the fire.

"They burned down his castle," she said simply. "They destroyed everything that the count owned, so that there was no reason for him to want to leave his grave. So now the fort is just a ruin at the top of the mountain, and we no longer have a count."

"But it didn't work," said Anna slowly. "Mrs. Dalca knew that it didn't. She still stays inside at night, and she feeds you garlic every day. What else does she do?"

Isabella thought about it. "She calls storms like this *strigoi furtună*. I thought she just meant the sound of the wind." She saw the look of confusion on Anna's face. "In Romanian, *strigoi* doesn't just mean vampire. It also means the noise you hear when somebody screams."

Scream storms. Vampire storms. Anna glanced out the main window. The weather had been horrible ever since they arrived on the mountainside— almost unbelievably so. Now it seemed as if they might know why.

"So vampires can control the weather," she said. "That's great news. Anything else?"

Isabella shook her head. "I think that's everything."

Anna remembered the bear sleeping in her room. "I bet they can control animals too. Mrs. Dalca must not know about that one."

"I guess not," said Isabella.

Anna considered everything that Isabella had told her. "So if the vampire is the old count, it probably still lives in the burnt castle. That's where it's taking Max. Do you know how to get there?"

"I've never been that far up the mountain," said Isabella. "But I can show it to you on a map."

She ran back to her bedroom. Anna sat alone in the kitchen. The hopelessness of the situation was starting to nibble away at her courage. The vampire was a powerful monster, lurking in a fortress in the midst of a magical storm. If fire hadn't been enough to stop the vampire rising, what could two children do to defeat it? And then there was the most chilling thought of all: what if they went all the way to the castle, only for the vampire to capture them as well?

"Here you go," said Isabella, reappearing at the doorway. "I brought your knife."

Anna tried to look her bravest. She took the knife from Isabella, squeezing the ever-warm handle in her palm. Suddenly she *felt* brave.

Isabella unrolled the map, holding the edges against the floor.

"This is where we are," she said. It was an old map, covered in a mixture of printed text and small, neat handwriting. Most of the map was occupied by a great mountain range, with the word CAR-PATHIANS printed across. Isabella was pointing to a hand-inked square just beyond the boundary of the mountains, marked with the words WILD THYME INN.

But Anna wasn't looking at the inn. She had seen a separate note, scrawled in the center of the vast woodland area: LIBRARY. The library was many miles away from the inn—many miles away from everything. The Professor was even farther away than she had thought.

Isabella was busy tracing her finger along the map, following a line so thin and faded that it must have been drawn on with pencil. Her fingertip crossed over a river and stopped at the top of a high hill, tapping importantly.

"That's it," she said. "That's the castle. It's got the heraldry and everything."

A marker in the shape of a shield had been printed at the hill's peak. Anna tore her eyes away from the faraway library to look at it.

She gasped. The shield was emblazoned with a tiny bird, its wings spread out on either side. In its talons was the crescent moon, stolen from the night, or even from a brave girl's cheek.

Now Anna had all the puzzle pieces that she

needed. She froze, her mouth open, mentally connecting all of the dark and dangerous dots.

"That symbol…" she said. Isabella looked at her curiously. Anna gathered her thoughts.

"The people living in the forest had to burn everything the count owned to stop him from becoming a vampire," she said quickly. "But he turned into one anyway. So they must have missed something. Something the count owned must have survived the fire."

Isabella shrugged. "I guess so. But it could be anything."

Anna leaped to her feet. "There was a banner in my bedroom with an eagle on it, just like that one. It has to be from the castle. If we burn it, the count will stop being a vampire! We can end this whole thing now!"

She didn't wait for a reply. Anna sprinted down the hallway, the white knife swinging in her hand.

For the first time since they arrived at the inn she felt triumphant. The mystery was solved. There was nothing the vampire could do to stop them.

Anna threw open her bedroom door, ignoring the bear on the bed, staring expectantly at the floor where the eagle had been spread.

The banner was gone.

8

A SNAKE IN THE GRASS

ANNA PULLED ON A SPARE PAIR OF rainboots as Isabella fastened her coat. They found a pair of dusty flashlights in the storeroom, and filled their knapsack with spare batteries from the clock in the kitchen. They both took two cloves of garlic from the pantry, placing one into each of their pockets.

After that, their preparations were complete. The

two girls held hands as they opened the front door and stepped out into the storm.

Anna had braced herself for the cold, but she still gasped as the full force of the rain swept against her face. She pulled her hood down low, staring at the ground as Isabella led the way around the side of the inn. After only a few steps, she couldn't see the building behind them anymore. Anna kept her eyes on the path, which was practically a rabbit scratch amid the long grass of the field.

Soon they reached the outskirts of the forest, and now Anna could see no path at all. Tree branches whipped above them. The leaves were rustling so loudly that they might have been speaking, whispering secret words. It was the kind of forest that could swallow a child, easily luring them down false tracks and forgotten trails.

"Are you sure you know where we're going?" said Anna.

"Not really," said Isabella.

Anna took a deep breath. The girls stepped toward the trees, and then between the trees, and then they were in the forest, alone.

The path (if it could be called a path) was slick with mud and puddles. Hundreds of tiny streams were trickling down the slope, running around tree roots and fallen branches, weaving through the undergrowth. Every now and then one of the girls would slip, pulling at the hand of the other, and then they would both wobble and wave their arms to stop themselves from tumbling back to the bottom of the hill.

They trudged forward for half an hour when Isabella suddenly stopped. Anna looked up. She could only shine her flashlight on one thing at a time—the nearest tree, the nearest bush—but with every sweep she saw hints of the countless trunks and branches hidden in the shadows. The tree that stood before them now was a snaking mass of wooden arms, each one bristling up into the forest canopy. Every branch was coated with shaggy green moss, growing wild over the gray bark. Being near the tree made Anna uncomfortable. It looked like it had been the very first tree to grow on the mountainside—the original count of the forest.

"Let's keep going," she said.

But Isabella was biting her lip. She pointed to the ground.

"Look," she said.

Anna looked closely, shining her flashlight ahead. Her eyes eventually found the path—except now there were two paths. The track they were following split at the base of the great tree, branching off around the trunk in two separate directions. Where the paths led could not be seen.

"I don't know which way to go," said Isabella. "This wasn't on the map."

Anna didn't know either. She wanted to keep moving as quickly as possible, partly because she had just heard a rustling sound from the bushes behind them. It was not a noise that she wanted to investigate.

"The vampire must have come this way," she said. "Maybe it left footprints."

"Good thinking," said Isabella. "You check the left side; I'll check the right."

The two girls hurried forward, flashlights sweeping the forest floor. Anna's heart sank. The path was bumpy and overgrown, which already made things difficult to see. It seemed certain the rain would have washed away any clues.

"Have you found anything?" she called.

"Nothing," Isabella called back, her voice muffled.

And then Anna saw something. The thing was caught on a fallen twig, sagging down toward a puddle, shining red in the flashlight. For one horrible second, Anna thought it might be blood. She leaned down for a closer look.

It wasn't blood at all. It was something that made Anna very excited.

"Come and look at this!" she yelled.

Isabella came running around the side of the great tree. Anna held out the thing in her hand, her eyes gleaming.

It was a red gummy snake.

"Max had a whole bag of these," Anna said breathlessly. She thought about the breadcrumbs from the story she had told in the car.

If the trail was followed the other way, it would lead a person straight to Max.

"He left a trail for us to follow," said Anna. "Just like Hansel." She grinned. "He's going to lead us all the way to the vampire's lair."

There was another rustling in the long grass

nearby. The girls spun to face the sound, but a moment later the woods were still.

"Come on," said Isabella. She reached out her hand. "We better keep going."

Anna grabbed her palm. In her other hand she squeezed the white knife and the flashlight tightly between her fingers.

She couldn't shake the feeling that someone—or something—was following them.

The two girls hiked for another hour through the storm-soaked forest, searching for clues from Max's candy bag at each fork in the path. They were not disappointed. They found chocolate, caramel buds, jelly beans, marshmallows, and more. Anna was tempted to eat the clues, gooey as they were after lying on the wet ground, but she forced herself to resist. They might need to follow the trail back again when they wanted to return to the inn.

"I think we're getting close," said Isabella. "All we have to do is find the bridge over the creek, and then we'll be at the castle."

Anna nodded. She shined her flashlight onto their latest find: a red jelly bean. Red jelly beans were Max's favorites. If he was starting to throw them away, Anna knew he didn't have much candy left.

The rushing sound of the creek began to echo out of the darkness around them. The sound grew louder and louder, hissing away like the call of a colossal serpent, surrounding the girls and drowning out all other noises.

"Will the bridge be safe?" asked Anna uncertainly.

"I think so," said Isabella. "The stream isn't very big."

But Isabella was wrong. The stream had been gorging itself on stormwater, swallowing the rain until it was transformed from a babbling brook into a roaring river. When the girls finally arrived at the bridge it was almost completely submerged beneath the water. Only the two guide ropes stood clearly above the waves.

"Oh," said Isabella. "Well, it's lucky we wore our rainboots."

She said it in the same cheerful voice that the Professor used when he had to leave Anna and Max behind. Normally the falseness annoyed Anna, but now she found herself smiling.

"It is lucky," she said. "Maybe it'll be fun to splash our way through."

It helped to pretend that the adventure was just a game.

They decided that Isabella would cross first.

Anna shined her flashlight ahead as her friend stepped into the river, holding tightly to the guide ropes as she shuffled across the hidden bridge. Soon she was safely across, shaking her dripping feet on the distant riverbank.

"Your turn," she called, shining a light onto the river.

Anna reluctantly turned off her flashlight and placed it in her pocket. She went to put the knife away too, before realizing that it would probably slice through the bottom of her coat. She would be forced to hold on to it as she crossed—which meant that she only had one hand free to steady herself.

Anna tensed as she took her first step into the river. Her foot sank farther into the water than she had expected, which made her gasp; but then the sole of her rainboot connected with the bridge, steady beneath the torrent. It was difficult to hold on to the guide rope with only one hand. She wobbled slightly as she edged forward, moving as carefully as she possibly could. The white-tipped waves ran across her feet, seizing at her ankles, trying to pull her under.

She was halfway across the bridge when Isabella made a noise that was somewhere between a scream and a shout. Anna's head automatically shot up, which almost caused her to lose her balance; the hand holding the white knife waved desperately in the air as she tried to steady herself.

Isabella's face had gone very white. Her hands were trembling as they held the flashlight, which made the light on the bridge jump and flicker.

"What is it?" shouted Anna.

"It's nothing," called Isabella quickly. "Just keep moving."

Anna took another step across the bridge. "Tell me what's wrong."

"No," said Isabella. "It doesn't matter."

Her eyes kept darting between Anna's face and the space beside Anna's head, as if there was something interesting sprouting from her shoulder. Anna glanced down at her arm, wondering if a spider had fallen onto her from the treetops.

"No, don't look," said Isabella. "Don't look behind you. Just keep walking."

A chill ran its fingers down Anna's neck. She tried to keep staring at Isabella, taking one careful step after the next, slowly closing the distance between herself and the land. Isabella's face remained stricken. Now she was openly staring at the unknown thing, a thing that had made her eyes grow wide with fear.

Anna couldn't help herself. She looked back.

A pack of wolves was sitting on the bank behind her. They watched silently from the shadows, gray-brown fur ruffling in the wind. Their eyes were

She looked back.

small and yellow, each one sparkling with a hungry glint.

And then they began to howl. They threw back their heads and wailed into the sky, filling the night with their ghastly cries.

Anna ran. She let go of the guide rope and dashed recklessly across the bridge, plunging deeper into the swirling water with every step. Her feet began to slip and skid against the planks, splashing the water up and over the sides of her rainboots, but still she ran, charging toward the bank, which was now only a few feet away. Then her boot caught on a hidden snag and she tripped, and then she was falling face-first toward the icy water that would knock the breath from her lungs and carry her away.

But Isabella was there to catch her. Anna fell into her open arms, gasping. Together the girls staggered along the last few feet of the submerged bridge. Catching Anna had forced Isabella to drop her flashlight; Anna saw it sail away on the current, a glowing ship on the raging sea.

"Are they still there?" spluttered Anna. She sank to her knees. The ground was wet and muddy, but at least it was solid.

"Give me your flashlight and I'll check," panted Isabella.

The wolves had vanished. There were no signs on the far bank that they had ever been there at all.

"They might be looking for a different place to cross," said Isabella. "But now that we're over the creek, the castle should be just up ahead. As soon as we're inside, the wolves won't be able to get to us."

Sneaking into a vampire's lair suddenly sounded as appealing as it was ever going to get. Anna climbed to her feet, and the two girls kept walking.

It wasn't long before they came upon the ruined fort.

9

DROWNED RATS

THE CASTLE WAS A HALF-COLLAPSED MESS of blackened stone and wood. It seemed to be bent at dangerous angles, looming above the forest like a gigantic gargoyle. One of the walls had fallen in completely, bringing a side of the roof down with it. A single tower remained, tall and thin, swaying in the wind. The castle door had been torn away from its hinges.

The people who had set fire to the fort had done their job well. It seemed impossible that anyone—or anything—could live within this shell of a building. Anna couldn't see any lights inside. Had they come to the right place?

"Should we go in?" asked Isabella.

She shined Anna's flashlight into the open doorway. It looked as if the light was being sucked away into nothingness, lost forever in a black hole.

Anna raised the white knife, tensing her arm.

"Let's do it," she said.

The girls stayed close together as they walked into the first room. It was a small relief to finally be out of the rain. Anna shook the droplets from her jacket while Isabella shined the light around them. The room was empty, and the walls were completely bare.

"Nothing," said Anna.

"They tried to burn all of the count's possessions,

remember?" said Isabella. "It makes sense that there's nothing here."

But Anna refused to believe that the castle could be completely empty. "Let's find the tower," she said.

They walked farther into the ruins, soon finding the entrance to the castle spire. Anna saw with dismay that the wooden staircase had been burned away long ago, leaving behind only a pile of gray ash. The tower was nothing more than a hollow tube of stone.

"Don't worry," said Isabella. "There are still a lot of places Max could be."

The children searched room after room, climbing over fallen stones and ducking through crooked doorways, moving deeper and deeper into the castle. Their findings were the same: all the rooms were silent, abandoned, and empty. Anna's frustration began to grow. Had they come all this way for nothing? Had the vampire built a secret lair some-where else, in a place they would have no hope of finding?

Eventually there was only one room left. The old wooden door was still in place, though the lower half was riddled with holes. Anna's heart beat faster as they approached it. This was their last chance.

"We better get ready," said Isabella, shrugging the knapsack off her shoulders. She undid the straps and took out the thermos of garlic soup. "We need Max to drink this before the *strigoi* bites him. Then he'll be safe."

Anna wondered whether the soup-stew alone would be enough to keep Max—or them—out of danger.

"What if the vampire is in there with him?" she asked.

Isabella frowned. "You're right," she said. "What should we do then?"

Anna quickly thought about it. "If it doesn't look like Max is in danger, then we can hide and wait for the *strigoi* to leave," she said. "But if it looks hungry, one of us will have to distract it while the other one gets Max."

One of those jobs sounded a lot more dangerous than the other. With a sinking feeling, Anna looked at the thermos in Isabella's hands, and then at the knife in her own. It seemed like the decision had already been made for them.

"I'll distract the vampire," Anna said. The words were so terrifying that she barely managed to force them from her mouth. "You can take the soup to Max."

Isabella smiled reassuringly. "You already ate some garlic, remember? The *strigoi* won't be able to bite you."

But what else could it do? The vampire had already sent a bear to attack her. How else could it harm her without needing to drink her blood? Anna shuddered. It was probably better not to think about it, but that was all she seemed able to do.

Isabella took off her scarf and tied it around the flashlight so that only a small amount of light shined from the end. Then the girls tiptoed to the door. Isabella put her fingers on the handle and nodded at Anna, and Anna understood that the nod meant *get ready*.

The door swung open.

Immediately there was movement in the room beyond. Isabella switched off the flashlight. Anna froze, trying not to move a single muscle. She was listening intently, but the only sound coming from the room was a quiet rustling. She hoped it was Max. She wished that he would say something, to let them know he was safe, or to tell them where the vampire was hiding.

But nothing happened. The girls stayed poised

at the entrance to the room, unmoving, listening to the rustling. It almost sounded like birds cheeping.

Isabella switched the flashlight back on and held it close to her face. "*What do we do?*" she mouthed.

"*Shine the flashlight in,*" whispered Anna. "*Let's see what it is.*"

Isabella nodded and pointed the flashlight through the doorway. She began to unwrap her scarf, gradually allowing more and more light to enter the room.

And then Anna saw it: a pair of eyes, glowing in the light. Then she saw another pair, and then another. Suddenly the room was filled with them: hundreds and hundreds of tiny white eyes.

"Oh no," she said.

The floor of the room was covered with mice—and now they had been disturbed. The rodents ran around the room in a panic, clambering over one another as they tried to escape, blindly searching for an exit. They soon discovered there was only one way out: through the door the girls had just opened.

Anna tried not to squeal as the first wave of mice scurried over her feet. They poured out of the room like dirty water, flooding the corridor with their small, soft bodies. Some of them massed into squirming piles, climbing up the backs of the girls' legs and falling into their rainboots. Anna frantically tried to swat them away. For every mouse she slapped, another would rise from the pile to take its place. The feeling of their wriggling fur was completely disgusting.

It took a whole minute for the room to empty. The girls spun around like clumsy ballerinas as they struggled to knock the mice away. Eventually the last mouse ran past them, a final drop in the hairy river.

"That was horrible," gasped Isabella. She shook her arms in repulsion, as if the sensation of tiny mouse paws was lingering on her skin.

"They must have come in here to get away from the storm," said Anna. "It's probably the driest place in the entire forest."

Isabella was still shaking. Anna took the flashlight from her and shined it into the mouse room. Now that the rodents were gone she could see that the floor was covered with mottled red carpet. It was the only place in the castle where the stone floor was not exposed.

"None of the other rooms had carpet, did they?" Anna said. "Maybe that's a clue."

She stepped inside. The room seemed better preserved than most of the others they had searched through, but it also looked as if the walls had been damaged from the inside. Huge flakes of stone had been broken away, giving the room a scarred, ragged appearance.

Anna looked at the walls closely. One area in the corner hadn't been scratched as badly as the rest. It looked like a picture had been carved into the wall, long before someone had come along to destroy it. Anna traced her fingers over one of the delicate lines. It might have once been the end of an eagle's claw.

"The count must have put his crest on the wall," said Isabella, who had followed Anna into the room. "And the people who live in the woods tried to take it off again." She sighed sadly. "They tried so hard to stop this from happening."

Anna turned back to face the empty room. "But where's the vampire? Where's Max?" She stamped her foot. "We've been through the entire castle now, and we haven't found anything!"

She stopped. Isabella had a funny look on her face.

"Do that again," she said.

Anna was confused. "Do what? Complain?"

"No, not that," said Isabella. "Stamp your foot!"

Anna stomped on the floor. A small puff of dust rose from the carpet, filling the air with the smell of mice. But this time Anna heard it as well: a creaking noise directly beneath her foot. She tapped her heel firmly on the ground. It sounded like she was banging on a squeaky drum.

"That doesn't sound very solid," said Isabella.

Anna bent down and grabbed a handful of carpet. It lifted up easily as she dragged it away from the wall, exposing the gray-white stone beneath— and something else too. A wooden square had been concealed under the shaggy red rug. A thick iron ring was attached to the top, almost like a door knocker.

It was a trapdoor.

"It looks like there's still some castle left to explore," said Isabella.

Anna nodded. She grasped the iron ring and pulled on it as hard as she could.

The trapdoor swung open. The girls leaned over the hole. A stone staircase stretched down into the earth, following a tunnel that was as dark as dark could be. Water was leaking down the walls, trickling out of cracks in the foundations of the castle. The whole place smelled stale and musty, like a tomb that should never have been opened.

Anna knew she had to go inside, even though she didn't want to. She knew Isabella must be feeling the same way.

"Are you sure you want to do this with me?" Anna asked.

Isabella smiled nervously. She placed the thermos back in the knapsack and took out the rope instead, tying it around the metal ring.

"This is the most scared I've ever been in my life," she said. "But we don't have any choice, do we? Max is your brother, and you're my friend."

Anna had only known Isabella for less than

a day, but so far they had chased a vampire up a mountain, escaped from a pack of wolves, and avoided being eaten by a horde of mice. She decided that Isabella might be the best and most interesting friend that she had ever had.

"I'm glad you're here with me," Anna said.

Then the girls took hold of the rope and stepped down into the tunnel, closing the trapdoor behind them.

10

THREE KEYS

IT FELT LIKE THEY WERE BEING EATEN. The tunnel was like a throat, dark and dripping with saliva, slowly leading them into the stomach of a great beast. The stone staircase was long, slippery, and treacherous, and more than once the girls slipped and fell, dangling helplessly from the rope until they could regain their footing.

The sounds of the storm had finally been muffled

by the layers of castle standing above them. The sudden silence was chilling. Anna flinched at every sound, scared by a drip of water or the echo of a footstep. She tried to focus on the plan. She would distract the vampire, and Isabella would get the soup to Max. Then they could all escape, and they would never have to return to the creepy old castle for as long as they lived.

Isabella stopped abruptly. Anna skidded into her back, almost knocking her over.

"Sorry," Anna whispered. "Why have we stopped?"

Isabella pointed to the ground. Anna saw that they had reached the foot of the staircase. Sitting on the last step was an empty brown paper bag.

Anna picked up the bag and tipped it onto her hand. Some small white crystals fell out from the deepest creases of the paper, sprinkling onto the center of her palm. She tested them with her tongue.

"It's sugar," she said. "This must be where Max ran out of candy."

"He must be close," said Isabella. "This tunnel can't be *that* long."

The girls stood nervously in the darkness. As short as they hoped the tunnel might be, it was still long enough that they couldn't see the end.

They began to creep forward.

"Do you think this was a cellar?" asked Anna. "Or was it a dungeon?"

Isabella frowned. "Whatever it was before, it's definitely a dungeon now."

Anna squinted, trying to see farther. Where would they find Max? Would he be chained to the wall? Or would he be trapped in a cage like Hansel in the witch's house, waiting to be fattened up with gingerbread before the monster ate him?

Something flickered in the distance. Anna saw there was a bend in the tunnel ahead, with a faint orange light glowing out from around the corner. She gestured for Isabella to switch off the flashlight.

"Do you think this is it?" whispered Isabella.

"Maybe," said Anna. "Be ready for anything."

They sneaked toward the light, arriving safely at the bend. Anna put her hand on the wall and took a deep breath, flinching as the seeping water ran over her fingertips. She slowly leaned sideways, tilting her neck until she could see around the corner.

The tunnel widened into a small room, connected to a new passage that led into further darkness. The room contained a small table with a built-in drawer. There was a candlestick on top holding a burning candle—the source of the light. The flame was very still, burning calmly in its hidden home beneath the world. It looked like something was hanging above the candle, but from her current position Anna couldn't see what it was. There were no signs of Max or the vampire.

"Can you see anything?" whispered Isabella.

"Just a candle," Anna whispered back. "But don't turn the flashlight on yet."

The girls walked cautiously into the room. It was little more than an alcove, with the new tunnel opening uninvitingly before them. The tunnel looked drier than the last one, which Anna took as a sign that it might run even deeper.

"That candle is still pretty tall," said Isabella. "It probably wasn't lit very long ago."

She was right. A single bead of wax was running down the side of the candle, which was otherwise white and smooth. Anna walked up to the table and opened the drawer. It was filled with candles of all different shapes and sizes: tall ones, short ones, red ones, scented ones. There was even a small collection of birthday candles piled in one corner. Anna had assumed that the vampire could see in the dark. What did it need candles for?

She looked up. Just as she thought, there was something hanging on the wall—a row of keys. There were three of them hanging from iron hooks, evenly spaced, each one slightly different from the rest. At the end of the row was a fourth hook, but it was empty.

Isabella's eyes widened. "That's my key!" she said.

She pointed to the third key in the row. Anna looked at her in surprise.

"It was the key to our henhouse, back when we had chickens," explained Isabella. "But one night I accidentally left the key in the lock. The next day someone stole the chickens and the key, and they even took the lock as well."

Anna thought about it. "I bet the vampire stole all of them," she said. "And the candles too. It needs them to keep its prisoners locked up."

"How many prisoners do you think he has?" said Isabella.

Anna looked at the three keys again. "Not a lot. If it had to kidnap Max, maybe it doesn't have any left."

The metal hooks were high on the wall. Isabella climbed onto the table and collected the keys one by one. Anna remembered how tall and thin the vampire had been when she saw it through the window. It wouldn't have any difficulty reaching the hooks.

"So now we just have to find three locks," she said. "Simple."

"Simple," agreed Isabella, climbing back down. "Let's go."

The girls crept into the new tunnel. It was smaller than the last one. They were still able to walk along it easily, but Anna imagined that the vampire might have to stoop. Soon they came to a metal door built into the side of the passage. There was a strange lock attached to the handle, clearly out of place in the dark and dirty dungeon. It was golden and shaped like a love heart: the sort of lock a girl might use to protect her secret diary.

Isabella held out the keys. Anna picked out the smallest one, which was exactly the same golden color as the heart. She slid the key into the lock and turned. It opened with a small popping sound, dropping to the ground.

Anna pushed the door. It opened onto a tiny cell, dirty and uninhabited. There was a bucket of muddy water against one of the walls, and a tray in one corner that held something that might have once been food. Now it was just a mound of mold and black slime.

In the other corner there was a skeleton.

A scream tried to burst out from Anna's lungs. She struggled to keep it down, managing to reduce it to a whimper. Had they arrived too late?

Isabella was trembling, but she managed to speak. "That couldn't be Max," she said reassuringly. "It's too big."

Anna looked closely at the pile of bones. They were long and yellow-white, and clearly very old. She realized they couldn't possibly belong to her brother. Her heart was pounding in terrified bursts, but she still felt relieved.

"Okay. Let's keep going," she said. She didn't want to look at the skeleton any more than she had to.

They walked along until they came to a second door, this one bearing a large, rusty lock. Anna selected an equally rusty key from Isabella's hand and pushed it in. It turned awkwardly, sticking inside the keyhole, but after a forceful twist it also popped open.

The door swung open to reveal another cell, another bucket, and another tray. There was no skeleton this time. Anna wondered if the vampire had become so hungry that it had devoured an entire prisoner, bones and all.

The children kept walking. Anna wanted to start

running, but she forced herself to sneak forward crouching low to the ground, walking on her toes. Isabella stayed out in front, shining the light from wall to wall.

"There it is," she said, stopping just ahead of Anna. "That's my lock."

They had arrived at the final door, though it seemed that the tunnel continued for a little longer. Anna had no interest in exploring it more. The henhouse lock was silver and round, glinting from the darkness, ready to give up its treasure.

Anna took Isabella's key and opened the lock. It fell contentedly into her hand, happy to have been found again. It seemed like a good omen.

The door creaked open. Isabella shined the flashlight into the cell. There was another bucket, and another tray, but this time things were slightly different. The water in the bucket was clean and fresh. The tray was covered with strange vegetables, long and stringy. They didn't look as delicious as candy, but they might have been enough to feed a small boy.

However, the cell didn't appear to contain a prisoner. Anna stepped tentatively inside.

"Max?" she whispered. "Are you here?"

Isabella followed her in. "Max?" she called quietly. "Say something if you can hear us!"

And then something moved in the space behind the door. The girls spun around in alarm as a hand shot out of the darkness and grabbed onto Isabella's ankle, digging into her flesh with sharp, overgrown fingernails. Anna caught a glimpse of a wild face in the shadows, hairy and wrinkled, with bright, yellow eyes.

Then Isabella dropped the flashlight, and everything went black.

11

A FAIRY'S TALE

ISABELLA SCREAMED. ANNA HEARD THE flashlight clatter past her feet; she fell to her knees and patted the ground with her free hand, desperately searching for the light.

"Help me!" yelled Isabella. "Use the knife!"

The knife. Anna could sense its point in the air before her, as warm and as sharp as ever. But what could she do in the dark? It seemed too risky. What if she attacked Isabella by mistake?

And then a voice spoke from the shadows. It was very faint, croakier than even Mrs. Dalca's voice was.

"*What are you doing here?*" it said. The words curled around the cell like a wisp of smoke. "*Did you hide it? Is it safe?*"

Anna's hand brushed against the edge of the flashlight. She seized it and switched it back on, holding it out like a burning branch to keep the wild voice at bay.

There was a man lying against the wall of the cell, half-hidden behind the open door. His body was white, colorless except for an occasional speckle of green or gray. The hair on his head was faded as well, hanging around his pointed face like dying grass.

But scariest of all were the holes. The man's arms and legs were covered with hundreds of tiny puncture marks, each one evenly spaced across his skin. It looked like everything beneath the surface had been sucked away, leaving his flesh to sag from his bones like the rubber of an old balloon. The man looked almost as dead as the skeleton from the first cell.

But the man's yellow eyes were still open, and his fingers were still closed around Isabella's leg. Anna saw that Isabella had bitten down on her scarf to stop herself from screaming anymore. The man was staring at Isabella furiously, as if he recognized her. Then the man looked at Anna, and at the knife in her hand. His eyes flickered.

"*Who are you?*" he said again.

Anna felt compelled to answer. She was about to speak when the knife suddenly pulsed with heat, tingling against her palm. She gasped, looking down at it in surprise. Somehow the shock made her feel less afraid, and she began to think more clearly. The man's eyes were far too yellow, and the words spoken by the whispering voice crept around her ears in a way that wasn't normal. The person in the cell was not the vampire—but Anna realized he might not be a human either.

And if she wasn't dealing with a human, there might be rules she had to follow.

Do not accept food from a fairy. Do not tell a fairy your real name. If you are on a quest, do not tell a fairy where you are going or what you hope to do.

"My name is Rose," she said confidently. "And this is my friend, Violet."

Isabella shot her a confused look. Anna hoped that she wouldn't give them away.

"*Rose*," said the man (who might not have been a

man). The word fell from his mouth like a flake of snakeskin. "*Why have you come here, Rose?*"

"I'm happy to tell you," said Anna. "But first you have to let go of my friend."

The man seemed to consider it.

"*I could talk to you now, Rose,*" he said. "*But soon you will leave me, and I will lie here again, alone in the darkness. Why shouldn't I hold on to your friend, so I can talk to her forever?*"

The rules from the fairy-tale book scurried through her head. Anna tried to work out a way to escape without telling the man anything about their mission, but she couldn't think of anything else she had to bargain with.

"We're here to find the vampire," she said finally. "It stole my brother, and now we're going to rescue him."

The man remained silent. Anna searched for something else to say.

"If you let go of my friend, we could try to rescue you too," she said.

"*It is too late*," said the man. "*All of my blood has been stolen from me. I will never leave this cell.*"

Anna tried again. "If we do defeat the vampire, it won't come back. It won't be able to bite you ever again."

"*That is a nice thought*," said the man. "*But you will not defeat the creature that lives in this castle. It has grown too old, and it has grown too strong. Too strong for two little girls.*"

"We have garlic," said Anna. "It hates garlic. And we have this."

She held out the knife. It sparkled in the flashlight, its edge as thin as a razor. Anna noticed that the blade didn't even seem to cast a shadow.

The man's gaze was fixed on the knife. His eyes gleamed in their sunken sockets.

"*You do not know what that is*," he said.

Anna was starting to feel bolder.

"Maybe not," she said. "But I bet it's sharp enough to cut your hand off."

The man smiled. His lips were very thin, as white and dry as parchment.

"*Maybe it is*," he said. "*But maybe I'll be fast enough to catch your arm. And once I've got a hold of it, maybe I won't let go.*"

Anna looked at the man's free hand. She could see the finger bones under his skin, long and delicate. His fingernails had grown out like claws.

She decided to think of a different plan. She looked around the cell. The tray of strange vegetables caught her eye.

"Would you like some food?" she said. "I could move your tray closer."

The man didn't reply. Anna nudged the tray with the side of her foot, sliding it across the floor. She left it close enough to the man that he would be able to grab it and pull it closer, careful to keep her leg out of reaching distance.

The man sniffed.

"*This food is dead*," he said. "*But I can smell something I would eat. Something in your pocket.*"

What was in her pocket? Anna tried to think. Then she remembered—the cloves of garlic, stolen from the kitchen pantry. They were supposed to protect her from the vampire. Should she really give them to the fairy-man?

Isabella looked at her pleadingly. Anna realized that she didn't have a choice.

"Okay," she said. "It's a deal. If you let my friend go, you can have the thing in my pocket. Say it's a deal."

"*It is a deal*," said the man.

Anna passed the flashlight from one hand to the other, so that she was holding the white knife and the flashlight together in her right hand. She slowly lowered her left hand into her jacket pocket, keeping her eyes locked on the gaunt face in the shadows. Every story she had ever read told her that making deals with fairies was dangerous, and she was determined not to be tricked.

But then Anna was surprised. She had been expecting to feel the smooth husk of the garlic clove, but instead her fingers touched something else. It was something soft, furry, and warm: something that had sneaked into her pocket without her even knowing.

It was something alive.

Anna squealed and flung out her hand—and a mouse dropped from her pocket. It landed on its feet, standing perfectly still in the center of the room, unmoving but for its twitching whiskers. In the middle of a very confusing night, the mouse suddenly seemed to be the most confused of all.

And then the mouse bolted, scurrying frantically toward the darkness in the corner of the cell.

The man's arm was as fast as a snake. It shot out from his body so quickly that Anna barely saw it move, his fingers landing around the mouse like a cage of bone. The mouse began to squeak in terror, wriggling around in the man's hand, squeezing its head out between the man's knuckles. The man smiled.

"A strange thing to carry in one's pocket," he said. *"But if this is to be my last meal, let it be a feast."*

And before either of the girls could say another word, the man raised the mouse to his lips. Anna caught a glimpse of rotting teeth as his mouth opened, and a second later the mouse had disappeared. Its tail slipped between the man's lips like a piece of spaghetti.

"You are free to go," said the man.

His shackle-hand creaked open. Anna waited for Isabella to move, but she seemed to be petrified from shock. Anna took her hand and pulled her away from the man. She noted with some concern that the man's yellow eyes now seemed to be glowing a little brighter.

"*Our bargain is complete*," said the whispering voice. "*But I will offer you this advice for free. You should not stay here. This is not a place for children.*"

"We won't stay long," said Anna. "We'll rescue my brother, and then we'll leave."

The man made a gulping sound. Anna saw a bulge squirm down his throat, writhing beneath his wrinkled skin. She could still hear a muffled squeaking.

"*You should heed my advice,*" said the man. "*You are not the first who has tried to rescue a brother from this tower. It is not a story with a happy ending.*"

"Who was the first?" asked Isabella shakily.

"*A warrior,*" said the man. "*A great warrior, with*

140

a great weapon. He came to this forest to take back his brother. But the creature beat him down, and it drank from his veins, and then both brothers were lost."

Anna didn't know what to say. She looked down at the white blade. *A great warrior, with a great weapon.* When they had first entered the cell, she had thought the man might have recognized the knife—and then he had told her that she didn't know what it was. But if a great warrior couldn't defeat the vampire, what chance did they have? Then Anna remembered that the man had seemed to recognize Isabella as well.

"Why did you ask us if we had hidden something? What did that mean?" she said.

But the man wouldn't say anything else.

"Well, thank you for all of your advice," said Anna politely, giving up. "I'm sorry that the warrior couldn't rescue his brother. We're still going to try to rescue mine anyway."

Isabella leaned in closer to Anna's ear.

"But where do we look next?" she whispered.

"Oh," said Anna. She looked back at the man. "Do you know where the vampire might be keeping another prisoner?"

"*I have upheld my end of the bargain*," said the man. "*Any new words must come with a price. Do you wish to make a new agreement?*"

"But you never gave us anything," said Anna angrily. "You grabbed my friend when she wasn't yours to take, and then you told us not to do something that you knew we were going to do anyway. So you still owe us something. Tell me where my brother is."

The man snarled, and Anna took a step backward. His eyes had narrowed into reptilian slits, golden and deadly.

"*You would call me a cheat?*" he hissed.

The knife flashed hot.

"Yes, I would," said Anna. "Tell me where my brother is."

The man fell silent, brooding from the shadows. When he spoke again, his words were fast and soft, almost as if he didn't want the girls to hear him.

"*You have passed three doors already,*" he said. "*If you follow the passage outside it will lead you to the fourth and final door, beyond which is the largest cell of all.*"

"But we only found three keys," said Isabella. "We don't have a fourth one."

The man smiled then. It was an evil smile, full of pointed, decaying teeth.

"*Then someone must have already opened the door!*"

12

OPEN JAWS

THE MAN ON THE FLOOR COUGHED OUT A rasping laugh as Anna and Isabella hurriedly left the cell. Anna closed the metal door behind them, drowning out the man's wicked cackling.

"Should we lock it again?" asked Isabella.

Anna considered it. She remembered the way the man's face had twisted when she confronted him and the way his claws had dug into Isabella's skin. But the man had also seemed worried about them, telling them to leave the monster's lair for their own safety.

"I don't think he really wants to hurt us," she said. "Not while the vampire is around, anyway. If he escaped, he might try to help us."

Isabella rubbed her leg uncertainly. "Are you sure?" she said.

Anna wasn't, not really. She looked away from Isabella, staring down at the end of the tunnel that she had hoped they wouldn't have to explore.

"We better hurry," she said. "The man said that the vampire must already be down there."

Isabella nodded. "Okay. It'll probably be fine to leave it unlocked."

But as they kept walking Anna noticed that Isabella was looking behind them far more often than she had done before.

They had now traveled so deep beneath the surface that the passage was completely untouched by the storm. The ground under their feet was dusty, and the sides of the tunnel were dry. The walls had grown rougher; the stonework was now broken up with patches of white clay and crumbling earth, as if the castle was being left behind as they traveled to some strange, underground place.

"Look at that," said Isabella softly.

There was more firelight in the distance. It flickered out of a doorway at the end of the tunnel, a glow that was equal parts welcoming and terrifying. The old wooden door was already open, just as the yellow-eyed man had guessed. A small black key was sticking out of the lock.

With the light came a new sound, although it was a sound Anna had heard many times before. The sound was always quiet and sad, often hidden behind tear-streaked hands.

It was the sound of Max crying.

"He's here," she said. Hearing Max made her want to cry as well—but also smile.

"Don't get distracted," whispered Isabella. She switched off the flashlight. "We haven't rescued him yet."

Anna tried not to grin as they moved forward, pushing her excitement down so she could focus on the task at hand. She concentrated on the floor of the tunnel, solid and soundless beneath her feet. She felt like a living shadow, a phantom in the night.

They arrived at the doorway. Anna looked inside.

She gasped.

The fairy-man had told them that the fourth cell was the largest of them all. He was right. The room beyond the final door had been built into a cavern, with great stone stalactites hanging down from the ceiling like the teeth of the world. The roof was a flutter of activity, covered with furry bodies that

Anna thought might have been mice, or worse, rats; then one of the creatures spread its wings and uttered a chittering scream, and Anna realized that the ceiling was coated with bats.

A rocky staircase stretched down from the doorway to the floor of the chamber. Burning torches were strapped along the walls, casting eerie shadows across the cave, shining light onto the wooden table standing in the center of the room. Lying on the table was Max, alive and mostly well, his body tied to the table legs with rope.

Standing beside the table was the vampire.

Before now, Anna had only ever seen the monster when it was half-hidden in the rain. Now she could see it clearly, in all its deadly magnificence. It was tall, even taller than she remembered, and its arms were way too long, pointed and thin like the arms of an insect. The skin of its face was a pale

It was hungry.

gray. The rest of its body was hidden by shadows that were draped over its limbs like clothing.

But scariest of all were its fiery eyes. They glittered with magic light, glowering down at Max with a stare so fierce that Anna felt sure it would burn the boy. As strange as the eyes were, there was no mistaking the look on the vampire's face.

It was hungry.

Anna shuddered as she tiptoed down the staircase. She looked around the cave, trying to find something she could use to distract the vampire. She couldn't see any obvious solutions.

"What should we do?" she whispered.

There was no reply. Anna glanced over her shoulder, hoping Isabella was busy thinking of a good idea.

Isabella was gone.

And then Max screamed. It was the loudest scream that Anna had ever heard, wilder than any noise Max had ever made before. The scream echoed around the cavern in piercing waves; the bats detached themselves from the ceiling, disturbed by the shrieking, and suddenly the air was filled with the flapping of leathery wings.

The vampire had raised Max's hand to its mouth. Its jaws had opened wide, showing off the rows of teeth hanging from its pink gums. Each one of its teeth was perfectly shaped, curved and sharp like a tiny dagger.

Two of the dagger-teeth were now sunk into Max's flesh.

Anna watched in horror as the vampire's face changed from gray to pink, pink to red, growing darker and darker as it sucked away at her brother's blood. Max was twisting around on the table, desperately trying to break free of the vampire's grip, but not even his strongest heave could pull the vampire off balance. It stared at him greedily as it drank from his veins, its nose twitching, its cheeks now glowing a ruddy scarlet.

Anna gripped the white knife angrily. She wanted to attack the monster, fight it and beat it and kill it so that it could never hurt Max again. Rage rose up inside her. She felt like shouting a fearsome war cry and charging into the room, swinging her weapon around her head like a medieval knight.

But the knife was growing hotter and hotter beneath her fingertips. Anna wished she understood its powers. Holding it made her feel braver. It had helped her think clearly enough to bargain with the fairy-man. But what else could it do?

Without thinking, Anna raised a finger to the almost-invisible point of the blade. The knife had become so hot now that it felt like it was burning her palm, filling her body with a fire that rushed up her arm and into her chest, pumping through her heart. How sharp could the knife really be? Would it be strong enough to stab the vampire?

And then, without meaning to do it, Anna's arm

twitched. The knife slid easily into the tip of her finger. She gasped in surprise, unable to see the needle of air that her fingertip was impaled on. Quickly she drew the knife back. A teardrop of blood welled instantly from the puncture mark, fat and bright: a ruby-red jewel wobbling delicately on her skin.

Max stopped screaming. Anna's eyes shot back to the table. The vampire had ceased drinking, although blood was still dribbling down its chin. It raised its head, tilting back its chin, elevating its nostrils.

It sniffed.

And then its head turned toward the door.

Anna stared at the bead of blood running down her finger. She knew what the vampire had smelled. She watched from behind a rock as it dropped Max's hand and stepped away from the table, inhaling deeply, seeking out the intruding scent. The black shadow-clothes bound themselves more tightly to its spindly form as it moved, clouding around its body until only the fiery eyes were visible through the shroud.

Anna realized that if she didn't move quickly she would be forced to retreat up the staircase. Quickly she stole into the cave, ducking around the stalagmites and thick stone pillars that rose out of the floor. She couldn't hear anything behind her, but that wasn't any reason to slow down: she doubted that the vampire's footsteps made any sound.

Drip.

The droplet of blood had shaken loose from Anna's finger. It hit the ground with a tiny splash, dotting the ground where it fell. Anna glanced at her fingertip and saw that a new drop had already blossomed from the knife wound.

The new drop gave her an idea.

Anna reached out and dabbed her finger against a stalagmite as she passed it. Her fingerprint was pressed onto the stone like a stamp in red ink. At the next pillar she flicked a splatter of blood across the base, marking it with her color and her smell. Soon the cave was filled with dozens of bloody clues for the nosy vampire to discover.

Anna found a small recess to hide under, crouching beneath the rocky overhang. She could see shadows swirling in the opposite corner of the room, a sign that the vampire was following her trail. Max was still lying on the table. But where was Isabella? Anna hadn't seen her since she had first looked into the cavernous room. Had her friend really abandoned her?

And then Anna saw the firelight glint off something under the table. She squinted. There was someone sitting right below Max—someone who was notoriously good at hiding. A girl with wild black hair and a white moon-scar on her cheek was sawing at the ropes with her pocketknife, delicately slicing them away so as not to cut Max's skin. The metal thermos sat beside her, ready to protect Max with its soupy magic.

Anna breathed a sigh of relief. The two halves of the plan were coming together. If they could get out while the vampire was still distracted, the adventure would finally be over.

She turned her gaze back to the corner of the room. The shadows had stopped swirling. Where was the vampire now? Anna looked all around the cave, but she couldn't see where the monster might be. She glanced nervously at the table. Both of Max's arms were now free, but Isabella had only just started sawing at the ropes around his legs. They needed more time.

Anna checked her finger to see if it was still bleeding—and her eyes widened with shock. Blood was pouring from the tiny cut, dripping down into a small puddle that had formed at her feet. Even she could smell the blood now: it had the fragrance of an iron bar, a metal tang rising from a scarlet pool. She would have to move quickly if she wanted to avoid being found.

The stones were rough under her hands as Anna crawled out of the alcove. She moved slowly, looking carefully around the cave as she stood up. There were no moving shadows or burning eyes to indicate where the vampire was lurking. For one hopeful moment, Anna thought that maybe the monster had disappeared.

Then she felt a cold breath on the back of her neck.

Anna turned around.

The vampire was hanging from the side of the cavern wall, perched on the rocks like a praying mantis. It was so close that Anna could have reached out and touched it—or so close that *it* could have touched *her*.

Its face was split open with a blood-stained smile.

13

DEAD END

ANNA SQUEALED AS THE VAMPIRE SWOOPED down from the wall. It scuttled onto the stony floor like a spider, its eyes burning brighter than the sun, hungry and enraged. Shadows wound around its gnashing teeth, billowing out of its mouth like smoke.

Anna backed away slowly. She held the white knife in front of her, aiming the tip directly at the vampire's head.

"Stay back!" she said.

She remembered how the bear in her bedroom had obeyed her commands when she had pointed the knife at it. Would this monster do the same?

The vampire stared for a moment at the blade that hung in the air between them, tilting its head thoughtfully. Then it lunged forward, its arm shooting out so fast that Anna didn't have time to react. Its hand connected painfully with Anna's wrist; the white knife was knocked from her fingers, flying through the air and clattering uselessly against a distant stalagmite.

"Oh," said Anna.

What could she do now? She continued to back away from the bloodthirsty beast, trying not to trip over the rocks on the ground. If she tripped now, she might never get up again.

"Hey!" called a voice from the other side of the cavern.

The vampire jerked its head toward the noise. Isabella was standing at the foot of the staircase, turning the flashlight on and off in distracting bursts. Beside her was Max, freed from his bonds and looking only slightly shaken.

"Run, Anna!" yelled Isabella. "Let's get out of here!"

The vampire spun back around, arms ready to strike, but Anna was already running for her life. She darted across the cave, weaving in and out of the pillars, glad to put some obstacles between her and the monster. She could hear the vampire clearly now. It rustled through the air as it moved, whistling like the wind as it pursued her through the darkness. Even though she was running very fast, she could tell that it was close behind her.

And then Anna made a mistake. She turned around the side of a stalagmite and ran straight into a wall—a dead end in the wrong corner of the cavern. Isabella and Max were climbing up the rocky stairs above her, incredibly close and yet too far away for them to lift her up. Anna turned around, ready to sprint to the foot of the stairway.

The vampire stood silently before her, blocking her path. It had positioned itself carefully this time, deliberately spreading its long limbs so that there was no way to pass it. Anna pressed herself against the wall, breathing heavily. The exit to the cave was directly above her. Did she have any chance of climbing up the wall before the monster could grab her?

"*Alo! Strigoi!*" yelled Isabella.

Anna looked up to see her friend's face peering over the ledge. The vampire looked up too, snarling angrily.

"I stole your dinner!" called Isabella. "You must be hungry! So here! Have some of this!"

And with that, she poured the contents of the metal thermos onto the vampire's face.

The vampire howled in pain. The soup-stew hissed and sizzled as it splashed against the monster's flesh, melting the skin away from its cheeks and chin. Its shadow-clothes twisted furiously around its hands as it tried to scrape the soup away. It fled, dragging itself back into the murky depths of the cave.

"Come on, Anna!" yelled Isabella. "Get up here, quick!"

Anna turned to run, happy to finally escape the vampire's clutches—but then something caught her eye. The white knife was glimmering in the firelight, half-hidden among a pile of nearby stones. What would happen if the weapon was captured by the evil creature? Anna changed direction mid-step, running toward the blade.

"*What are you doing?*" yelled Isabella. She stood with Max in the doorway, ready for their flight to freedom. Anna hoped she wasn't ruining their one chance to get out safely. She scooped the knife into her hand and stood up, panting.

But then she saw there was something else under the stones. At first it looked like a shadow, except that it was blue rather than black. There were streaks of gold as well, woven into shapes that Anna immediately recognized: a moon, and a claw, and a beak. It was the eagle banner from her room, now buried in the depths of the vampire's lair—the one possession that had survived the fire, preventing the vampire from being destroyed forever.

"Anna! Come on!"

Anna quickly started shoveling the smaller stones off the top of the pile, straining her muscles to push away the largest rocks. If they could get the banner and burn it then the vampire would never be able to hurt anyone again. She dug furiously, scooping and digging and shoving. More and more of the fabric was slowly uncovered; soon she would be able to pull it out of its hiding place.

"*It's coming back!*" screamed Isabella.

A cloud of swirling shadows was approaching Anna. She grabbed a handful of the blue fabric and stood up, pulling with all her might. For a second the banner was trapped in place, weighed down by the remaining stones—and then with a sudden jerk it slipped free, and Anna was tumbling backward. She scrambled to her feet and ran for the staircase, the banner waving behind her like she was playing a game of capture the flag.

"Run!" called Max. "Faster, Anna!"

She could hear the whistling sound behind her as she clambered up the stone steps. Isabella and Max disappeared through the doorway, clearing the way for Anna to come through.

Anna could feel the cold breath on her neck. She tumbled through the doorway, and then:

BANG!

Isabella slammed the door as hard as she could. Max jumped forward and turned the key in the lock. There was a loud thump as something crashed into the wood on the other side.

"I don't think that will hold it for long," panted Isabella. "And there might be other ways out of that cave."

But for the moment, Anna didn't care about the danger they were still in. She didn't care that they were in a dungeon in a castle in a forest in a storm in the middle of Transylvania. All she cared about was that she had found Max. She threw her arms around him and gave him the biggest hug she had ever given anyone, even the Professor. Max hugged her back.

"Are you all right?" she asked him.

"Not really," said Max. "My hand feels really weird."

Anna took the flashlight from Isabella and shined it onto Max's hand. The two holes in his skin were perfectly round and alarmingly deep. But the scariest thing of all was the color. Max's fingers had turned as white as bone, tinged with the same gray-green as the skin of the fairy prisoner. Anna touched his palm. The skin felt cool and clammy. There wasn't any blood left in it.

Max's hand was dead.

Anna didn't know what to say. She watched as Max wiggled his fingers and scratched at his tufty brown hair.

"I can still move it," said Max. "But I can't feel anything. It's like it's not my hand anymore." He smiled sadly. "When you tell stories I always hope that nothing bad will happen to the Max character, but this time it really did."

Anna took his hand and squeezed it. "We'll find a way to fix it," she said. "I promise."

"Yes," said Isabella. "But we need to figure that out later. Because right now we really need to go!"

She pointed at the door. Smoky black tendrils were worming their way through the keyhole and around the hinges. The door was starting to tremble, shaking as if it might explode.

The children ran.

"I found the banner," explained Anna as they dashed past the third cell. (There wasn't time to check if the prisoner was still inside.) "If we can find a way to burn it, then we can finish what the forest people started. The vampire will be defeated for good."

"We can use the candle!" said Isabella. "It should be just ahead."

But when they reached the alcove they discovered that the candle had burned away to nothing.

All that was left on the table was a lumpy puddle of wax. They didn't see any matches.

"We'll have to get it back to the inn," said Isabella. "The fire in the kitchen should still be lit."

Max, having been kidnapped for most of the night, was becoming increasingly confused by the girls' conversation. They filled him in on everything that had happened as they ran down the last section of passage, passing the empty brown paper bag at the bottom of the steps. Anna noticed the unhappy expression on Max's face and almost laughed. Despite everything that had happened to them, Max was still sad about losing all his candy.

The children used the rope to help them climb up the slippery staircase, slamming the trapdoor closed when they reached the top. They'd hoped that the storm might have stopped during their time underground, but the sounds of rain and thunder roared as loudly as ever through the roof above.

If anything, the weather seemed to be even worse, growing in magnitude to match the vampire's fury.

They decided to abandon the rope. Anna led Isabella and Max back through the crumbling castle, walking delicately past the mice, which had started to regroup in the carpeted room. The children darted through the empty corridors and crooked doorways, their footsteps muffled by the scattered ashes that had once been the count's possessions. Soon they arrived back at the entrance room, stopping to catch their breath beside a large boulder. Anna took off her coat and wrapped it around Max, who was only wearing his pajamas. The cold air instantly made goose bumps pop up on her arms and neck.

"Is everyone ready?" she said. She stood in front of the open door, poised to step out. "One... two..."

Anna meant to say *three*, but at that moment

she saw something that made the word die in her throat. Isabella and Max stared at her, confused. She gasped, trying to speak—to warn them of the danger they were in.

The boulder behind Isabella and Max wasn't a boulder at all. It was something large and hairy, with arms and legs that were now unfolding from its body in the darkness.

The thing stood up, towering above the children, its claws long and sharp.

14

THE CHILDREN
OF THE NIGHT

ISABELLA YELPED AND JUMPED AWAY. MAX
stumbled forward, almost tripping as he hid behind
Anna. The thing growled, stepping in front of the
doorway, baring its teeth in the moonlight.

It was the second time Anna had seen a bear that
evening. She examined it closely, unafraid of the
animal while the white knife was in her hand. She
realized with surprise that she recognized its face.

"I know you," she said. "You're the bear from my bedroom."

The bear snarled. It dropped onto four legs and made its dog-lion roar, echoing in great booms around the castle walls. Max and Isabella covered their ears.

"Stop that," said Anna. She pointed the knife directly at the bear. "Sit down!"

"What are you doing?" asked Max. He sounded scared. Anna remembered that the others hadn't been there for her first encounter with the bear. She gave it a stern look, drawing herself up to her full height.

"Sit!" she said again.

The bear sat. It fell back onto its bottom with a dull thump, bowing its head as it had before. Isabella and Max exhaled loudly; both of them had been holding their breath.

"How did you do that?" asked Max.

Anna held up the knife. "I think it's afraid of this," she said. "It wouldn't work on the vampire or the fairy-man, but it's good for calming down bears."

The bear gave a rumbling purr.

"It seems nice, doesn't it?" said Isabella. "It probably didn't want to help the vampire."

Suddenly Anna had an idea. She looked at the bear's back, broad and muscled, curving down from its formidable shoulders. Apart from the fact that it was covered in hair, it was shaped almost like a saddle.

"I think I've found a way that the bear can make it up to us," she said.

Without waiting for the others to reply, Anna stepped right up to the bear's face. She held the knife loosely by her side, trying to be as friendly as possible as she stared into the small black eyes.

"Hello," she said. "Can you understand me?"

The bear didn't say anything. Anna had hoped that it would make noise, or at least nod its head, but she pressed on anyway.

"We need to get through the forest as quickly as possible," she said. "The monster that lives in this castle is chasing us, and if it catches us, then we won't be able to defeat it and it will keep making you do bad things. So, if it's all right with you, I was wondering if you could carry us on your back to the inn as fast as you can. Would that be okay?"

Anna said all of this as politely as she could, maintaining eye contact with the bear at all times. But it didn't move. It didn't even blink.

"This is a bad idea," whispered Max. "It can't understand what you're saying."

But then the bear kneeled down. It lowered its back as close to the ground as possible, sticking its great backside up into the air. It turned its head back to look at Anna, staring at her expectantly.

Climb aboard, it seemed to say.

A burst of light flared through the castle door-way as lightning struck the treetops outside. Thunder ripped across the sky with a fearsome bellow before the glow faded, rattling the foundations of the castle with alarming force. The noise electrified the children into action. Anna climbed up onto the bear's shoulders, holding on to the furry hump that rose up behind its head. Max scrambled behind her after Isabella gave him a boost, wrapping his arms around Anna's waist, and then Isabella leaped up as well, holding tightly on to Max, the eagle banner draped behind her.

The bear stood up. The children wobbled back and forth, squeezing their legs around the huge, hairy body. Anna positioned the flashlight so that it was shining between the bear's ears. It looked like a bizarre version of a miner's headlamp.

"Is everyone ready?" asked Anna.

"Yes," said Isabella.

"No," said Max.

Anna smiled, leaning forward so she could speak directly into the bear's fluffy ear.

"Let's go!" she said.

The bear shuffled over to the door. Anna could feel the animal's mighty shoulders moving beneath her, powerful and strong. She felt very glad that the bear was now on their side.

They stood still for a moment, surveying the forest. The trees were swaying dangerously in the storm, tipping so far to each side that Anna felt sure they would soon be torn from their roots. Branches were falling regularly from the sky, zipping through the air like broomsticks as the wind caught them and flung them from the canopy. The rain had become so cold that it might as well have been snowing.

Anna was about to suggest that they wait for a

break in the weather when the bear sprang into action. It charged fearlessly into the storm, digging its claws into the ground for traction as it bounded through the muddy puddles. All three children were thrown into the air; Isabella barely managed to keep holding on to Max, who barely managed to keep holding on to Anna, who barely managed to keep holding on to one small clump of the bear's fur. A falling stick whizzed past their heads, almost impaling them like a javelin. The leaves from low-hanging branches slapped against their faces, licking wetly at their cheeks. They rushed across the sunken bridge, cleaving the water into two great waves that splashed at their legs on either side.

"I feel sick," shouted Max. "I think we should get off."

"We can't get off!" called Isabella from the back. "We have company!"

Anna craned her neck to look behind them.

Dozens of gray-brown shapes were slipping through the trees on either side of the path, racing easily through the undergrowth. The creatures stuck to the shadows as they ran, but stray beams of moonlight sometimes gave away their positions, catching on a pointy ear or a long, bushy tail.

Then one of the shapes threw caution to the wind, bursting out onto the path behind them. A salivating tongue hung out over sharp white teeth as it snarled hungrily at the children.

"Wolves!" screamed Max.

Now the woods seemed to be filled with yellow eyes. The wolf on the path was running fast, getting closer and closer to the back legs of the bear; finally it leaped forward and snapped at the air, its jaws almost closing around the fluttering edge of Isabella's raincoat.

"Go away!" shouted Anna. She pointed the white

knife at the trees, waving it like a magic wand. "Stay away from us!"

The wolves kept coming; no matter how hard she tried, Anna couldn't point the knife in a straight line. The bear was running so fast now that it slipped and skidded at every turn, vaulting over fallen logs and crashing through bushes. It was the weirdest ride Anna had ever been on. If their lives weren't in so much danger, it almost would've been fun.

But now Anna wasn't sure of where they were. Every tree looked the same in the bobbing beam of the flashlight, shooting past in a tangle of twisted limbs. More wolves joined the first one on the path. They were closing in, running alongside the rump of the bear, getting ready for the final attack.

"Are we almost there?" she asked in a loud voice.

"Almost!" called Isabella. "The inn should be just up ahead!"

Anna had no choice but to trust that her friend was right. She leaned forward, pressing her lips against the bear's ear.

"You can do it," she whispered. "It's just a little farther."

The bear grunted.

The trees were starting to thin now, which meant that the wolves had fewer places to hide. The whole pack came together as one, moonlight shining off their ragged fur. They yelped and howled and barked as they pursued their prey, determined not to let their dinners escape.

Max swatted at a wolf with his dead hand, striking it across the muzzle. It fell back with a yelping noise, retreating behind its brothers.

"Got him!" said Max, pleased.

"Keep holding on!" said Isabella. "I can see it, just over there!"

Light was glowing dimly through the windows

"Wolves!" screamed Max.

of the Wild Thyme Inn. The white stone walls of the building stood solidly in the storm: a beacon of safety, shining through the mist and rain. The bear bounded out of the trees and galloped toward the inn, clambering across the back field. The children were sprayed with mud as it plunged through the slushy earth.

Anna looked behind them and saw with relief that the wolves had finally ceased their pursuit. Their gray-brown bodies lingered at the border of the forest, howling out their disappointment.

"All we have to do is get inside," she said excitedly. "Once we get that banner into the fireplace, this will all be over."

"Simple," said Max encouragingly.

"Not simple," yelled Isabella. "*Look!*"

The wolves had stayed in the woods, but something else had followed them out of the treeline. It was a huge, gangly shadow with spider-arms and fiery eyes, scuttling across the muddy field in a whirlwind of storm and fury. It opened its mouth and screamed at the children through gnashing teeth, a terrifying screech that flew at them on a breath of icy wind.

Anna and Isabella had stolen many treasures from the vampire that night.

Now it had come to steal them back.

15

CROSSING THE
THRESHOLD

THE BEAR RAN ALL THE WAY TO THE FRONT
of the inn, almost colliding with the warped wooden
door as it skidded to a halt. The children tumbled
off its back before it had even stopped moving.
Anna threw open the door and rushed inside, followed closely by Max; Isabella came in last, the
eagle banner dragging behind her. To Anna's surprise, the bear came in also. Once inside it shook its

body back and forth with great gusto, spraying the dining room with water and mud.

"Get the banner to the fire!" said Max.

The two girls ran to the fireplace—and saw with dismay that the fire had almost gone out. Only a small pile of blackened embers remained, glowing a dull red among the gray ash. Anna tried to throw the banner on top of them, but Isabella pulled it back.

"The fabric is soaking wet!" she said. "If we put it on now it'll just extinguish the embers. We'll have to get the fire burning properly before we can put it on."

Anna dropped the white knife and took the banner from Isabella, wringing it between her hands. Hundreds of fat water droplets fell out onto the floor, and Anna realized that her friend was right. Isabella kneeled by the fire and grabbed some sticks from the pile of wood she had brought inside, snapping them up and dropping the pieces onto the coals.

"We might need the paper on that shelf," said Isabella, pointing. "Max, can you roll some up into little balls?"

Max nodded. He had been staring sadly at his lifeless fingers; now he ran to the shelf and began tearing up the paper, scrunching it with his good hand. Anna kept squeezing out the water. She hadn't noticed how wet the banner—and her clothing—had become during their ride in the storm.

A tiny flame crept out from the coals. It wavered timidly below the pyramid of twigs Isabella had built in the fireplace, tickling the bottoms of the sticks. Anna and Isabella stared it at intently, willing the flame to blossom into a mighty blaze.

"*It's here!*" said Max in a terrified voice.

The vampire was standing outside the inn's window. Its glare was brighter now than ever before, sparkling so ferociously that the flaming eyes seemed to engulf the vampire's entire face. Anna squashed the banner between her palms again and again, frantically trying to dry it out. Isabella was focused on the fire, giving the vampire only the briefest of glances.

"Why isn't it coming inside?" she asked.

"I have no idea," said Anna.

"Vampires can't cross the threshold of a house without being invited," said Max quickly.

Anna looked at him, surprised. "Who told you that?"

Max shrugged. "I read it in one of your books once."

"How did the vampire kidnap you, then?" asked Anna.

"It reached through the window," said Max. "I guess that's allowed."

Anna stared out at the vampire, trapped behind a pane of glass. She grinned. "Well then, if we stay away from the window, the vampire can't get us," she said. "And that means we can take as long as we want to get this fire started. We win!"

But as she kept staring at the vampire, the grin quickly melted off her face.

Because now the vampire was smiling as well.

"My hand!" said Max suddenly. "I can feel it! The blood must be coming back in!"

Anna spun around to face Max. He was wiggling his fingers delightedly, curling them in the air as if he was playing a piano. But something was wrong. His skin was even whiter than before, the color of broken eggshell or the driest of bones: a color skin most certainly should not be. And now there was something else too.

Max's hand was glowing.

Suddenly his fingers snapped into a fist. They clenched themselves tightly, knuckles pointing outward, his thumb curled around to the front. "Hey," said Max, confused. "I didn't mean to do that."

His arm started to tremble. Anna realized he was trying to stop the fist from moving. She watched, shocked, as the dead hand punched out from his body. It started floating across the room, dragging Max behind it.

"I can't control it!" spluttered Max. He grabbed his wrist with his good hand, straining as much as he could. "I don't know what's happening!"

"It's the *strigoi!*" said Isabella. "Look!"

The vampire had raised one of its own hands up to the window pane. Its long fingers were dancing in the misty air, spinning around in weird and intricate patterns. It looked like it was controlling an invisible marionette. The vampire's lips were also moving. Anna watched them closely, and for one moment she heard a string of strange words that felt terrible in her ears.

And in that moment, the eagle banner was snatched from her hands.

Anna whirled around. The blue fabric was now clutched in Max's white-knuckled fist.

"*What are you doing?*" she exclaimed.

The dead hand picked up its pace, surging across the room toward the window. Max dug his heels into the floorboards, trying to stop the hand's progress; the hand struggled with such force that he was nearly pulled over.

Anna grabbed the trailing end of the banner, pulling it back toward the fireplace. The hand—and Max—spun around to face her.

"Let go!" she yelled.

"I can't!" whimpered Max.

The hand tugged rapidly at the banner, almost succeeding in wrenching it through Anna's fingers. Anna quickly took hold of her end with both hands, tensing her arms and legs. The banner went taut, stretched between the two siblings.

"You can't have it!" Anna shouted at the window.

"We stole it, and now we're going to burn it, and then all of this will be over! There's nothing you can do about it, so give up!"

The dead fingers opened.

Anna had been pulling on the banner with all her strength, so the sudden release sent her flying backward. She stumbled, falling over and hitting her head against the leg of the table. A sharp pain shot out from just above her ear, ringing through her thoughts. Had she really just convinced the vampire to give in? Was it really prepared to accept its fate and let them burn the banner? Anna tried to look around, but her eyes were watering, blurring her vision. She sat up, blinking away tears.

And then Max punched her in the nose.

Anna fell to the ground. She looked up woozily to see Max standing above her, his fingers waggling, stretching themselves after the blow.

"I'm sorry," Max whispered. His mouth was

hanging open, horrified at what he had just done. "I would never mean to hit you. Never, Anna."

But even as he said it, the hand was already pulling him down, ready to strike again. It changed direction at the last moment, swiveling toward the banner instead. Anna watched as the cold fingers seized the fabric, drawing it away from her.

Anna didn't think she could stand up right away. She turned her head to look at Isabella, hoping she could save them, but Isabella remained focused on adding wood to the fireplace. Then her eyes fell on the white knife, only a few feet away. Anna rolled across the floor to it, desperately reaching for its leather-wrapped handle.

The windowpane shattered. The air was filled with smithereens of glass as the storm winds rushed inside. Max had almost reached the vampire. The monster stretched its spider-arm through the broken

The windowpane shattered.

window, ready to receive the one thing it needed to stay alive.

Anna's fingers closed around the hilt of the knife.

"Bear!" she yelled. "Get the banner!"

The spell hadn't worked when she'd tried it on the wolves—would it work now?

To her great relief, Anna heard the scuffling sound of paws as the bear charged forward. It chomped its teeth down on the trailing end of the banner, hauling Max away from the window. The bear shook its head back and forth, trying to wrestle the banner from the dead hand. The banner began to shake loose, slowly slipping through the deathly grip.

And then Isabella appeared at the bear's side. She added her weight to the tug o' war, and with one final pull, the banner flew free.

"Thanks!" she said, grinning.

Anna looked at the fireplace. A roaring fire was burning in the hearth.

The vampire screamed. Its arms seemed to lengthen as it lunged through the smashed window, stretching out to impossible proportions, swiping furiously at the children.

Isabella dropped the fabric onto the flames.

It must have been a beautiful banner, once upon a time. The sky looked clear and limitless; the eagle was proud and majestic, strong enough to carry the moon itself in its golden talons. For a moment, the great bird shone brighter than ever as the orange sparks wove their way between the fibers, transforming the eagle into the phoenix of legend, its feathers ablaze. Then the fire took root, and the eagle was burned to black, and the final possession of the count on the mountain was eaten away.

The vampire had stopped screaming. It seemed to be frozen in place. Anna watched as its white eyes winked away, as if the rain had finally succeeded in snuffing out its fury. Shadows swirled around its arms, which were still reaching through the window—and then Anna blinked, and suddenly it was only shadows that remained where the vampire had stood, floating harmlessly around the walls of the inn.

Max had fallen against the bear. They sat together on one side of the room; Max was still staring out of the empty window, his hand seemingly back under his own control. Isabella was slumped against the fireplace, breathing heavily, her face stained with smoke. Anna took hold of the table leg and dragged herself up.

The three children stared at one another, none of them speaking a word.

The clouds in the sky vanished as one, taking with them the mist and the winds and the rain. The first rays of sunlight peeked over the horizon, shining through the window, filling the room with a warm radiance.

It was a new day.

16

PARTING GIFTS

FOR THE REST OF THE MORNING, THE children slept. They curled up together in Isabella's bed, peaceful and safe, dreaming pleasant dreams. When they woke up the sun was high in the afternoon sky. Mrs. Dalca was bustling around the front room, sweeping up the broken glass with a straw-bristled broom.

"*Isabella!*" cried the old woman upon seeing the children.

Isabella ran to her grandmother, who immediately swooped her into a loving embrace. Anna watched the two of them hug, feeling bad that she had once suspected Mrs. Dalca was a witch.

"We've had the biggest adventure, Granny," said Isabella. "We walked all the way to the old count's castle, and when we went inside…"

"*Nu vreau să știu!*" interrupted the old woman. She raised a wrinkled hand and traced a pattern in the air.

Isabella looked up at her, puzzled.

"But, Grandma, Max got taken in the night. We had to go and fight…"

Mrs. Dalca covered her ears.

"*Nu-mi spune acest lucru,*" she croaked. "*Mă va pune în pericol!*"

"What is she saying?" asked Anna.

Isabella frowned. "She says she doesn't want to know. She says it'll put her in danger."

"How come?" said Max.

"I'm not sure," said Isabella sadly.

They watched as Mrs. Dalca shuffled away with her broom, sweeping at the shadows in the corner of the inn.

The children decided to go for a walk. They had let the bear out of the inn before they fell asleep, and now they hoped to find it so they could thank it for its help. Isabella had taken two red apples from the pantry to give to the bear as a gift. Anna held the white knife by her side, just in case.

It was a beautiful day. The children raised their faces to the sun, enjoying the touch of warm light on their cheeks. Wildflowers were blooming in the back field, speckling the grass with bursts of purple and blue and red. The air smelled sweet and fresh.

As they walked along, they compared each of the new scars they had received on their adventure. Isabella had a mark on her ankle from where the fairy prisoner had held her. It was shaped, appropriately, like a handprint: the skin was red and swollen, almost like she had been burned. Anna's best new scar was the one she had accidentally given herself with the point of the knife. The tip of her finger was now wrapped in a bandage, applied by Isabella the night before. The cut was taking an unusually long time to heal.

Both girls agreed, however, that the most impressive injuries of all were the two puncture wounds in Max's hand. They made a big deal about this, and Max began to feel proud of his new, strange, dead hand. He waved it through the air as they strolled across the field, showing it off as much as he could.

They found the bear at the edge of the forest, reclining lazily in the shade of a tree. Sitting against the tree was a tall, thin man with a tangle of gray hair cascading around his pointed face. His clothing was a strange mixture of green and gray, as if the fabric had been woven from leaves and ash. It hung from his skin like a coat of scales, shimmering in the breeze.

"Who are you?" said Anna.

The man opened his eyes, and Anna knew at once whom she was speaking to. The eyes were just as bright and yellow as the first time she had seen them.

"*Hello, Rose,*" said the prisoner from the castle.

Max opened his mouth to say something, confused; the girls hadn't told him about their secret names. Anna quickly stepped on his foot.

"Hello," she said confidently. "It looks like you got out."

The ex-prisoner ran a hand across the bear's shaggy head. It growled contentedly.

"*I have had a very fortuitous day,*" he said. "*An unexpected meal. An unlocked door. A rope to help me up the steps. And now it seems as if the creature from the castle has been defeated, once and for all.*"

"Yes, it has," said Anna. "You're welcome."

The fairy-man frowned.

"*This was not a job for children,*" he said. "*Humans should not meddle in the affairs of the old wood.*"

"The vampire meddled with us first," said Anna. "So there."

The yellow eyes twinkled. Anna wasn't sure if the man was angry or amused.

Isabella kneeled down and held one of the apples under the bear's nose. It sniffed curiously at the fruit before taking a large bite, crunching the white flesh between its teeth. It seemed pleased with the present.

"*What will you do with the knife?*" asked the man.

Anna hadn't thought about it. She glanced down at the blade in her hand. It was glimmering silver in the sunshine, reflecting the light so brightly it almost hurt her eyes.

"I'm not sure," said Anna. "What do you think I should do with it?"

The fairy-man tilted his head.

"*There will he consequences to keeping it,*" he said. "*For it is not a thing that should be held by human hands. There are monsters in the world far worse than the creature that dwelled in these woods, and their attentions would certainly be drawn to a weapon such as this.*"

"How did it get in my granny's inn, then?" asked Isabella, patting the bear behind the ears.

The fairy-man closed his eyes. When he spoke again, Anna was struck by the tenderness in his voice—a world apart from the cold, rasping words he had spoken in the cell.

"*A young traveler brought the knife to this forest,*" he said. "*He was a great warrior, who had hoped to free the monster from its curse by entering its lair and destroying its last token of life. He succeeded in beating back the beast and finding the flag, but in doing so he received a grave wound. He staggered back through the woods, knowing that the creature would soon be upon him.*"

"That's a lot like our story," said Max. "Except this one doesn't sound like it will have a happy ending."

The man gave a cold smile.

"*The traveler met a young girl in the woods, and he thrust the knife and the banner upon her, for he did not want either of them to fall back into the hands of the beast. Then the monster caught him, and bit him, and dragged him back to the dungeon beneath its castle. It drank from his veins every day for sixty years, until there was no blood left to be stolen."*

Anna and Isabella had heard a shorter version of this story before, back in the vampire's lair—except the last time the man had told it, he had said the traveler was searching for his brother. Anna remembered the hundreds of bite marks she had seen across the man's arms and legs. She remembered something else too: a line from her book of fairy tales.

When a fairy dies, their magic does not always die with them. The trapped magic can sometimes transform their body into an entirely different creature.

"You were the traveler," said Anna, slowly working it out. "And the vampire used to be your brother."

"And the little girl must have been Granny

Dalca," said Isabella. "That's how the knife ended up at the inn. If she'd only known what the banner was, she could have ended all this years ago."

Anna tried to imagine the scene the man had described. She pictured a little girl with gray-white hair running through the forest at night, trying not to scream as she listened to the cries of the wounded man she had left behind. Had the floorboard in the bedroom always been loose, or had the girl ripped it open so she could hide the knife in a secret place? And why hadn't she hidden the banner with it? Anna supposed that it must have looked too pretty to stow away in the dark.

The man was now regarding the children in silence. Anna shook her head, holding up the shining white dagger. Now she knew it had once belonged to the fairy. Did that mean she would have to give it back to him?

"*I will not ask for the knife*," said the man, reading

her thoughts. "*I have no further use for it. But I will take it from you if you wish, should you not want to be burdened with its ownership.*"

Anna turned to Isabella and Max. "What do you think we should do?"

"Give it back," said Max.

"Keep it," said Isabella, almost at the same time.

Anna laughed. She raised the knife into the air, slicing sunbeams with its pale edge.

"We got attacked by a monster before we even knew the knife existed," she said. "What if that happens again? We might need some magic to help us."

Max groaned; Isabella nodded in agreement. Anna turned back to the fairy-man.

"We wish to keep it," she said.

The man reached into the pocket of his scaly coat. He pulled out a small scabbard made of the same green-gray material as his clothing, tied to a belt made of woven grass.

"*The blade is yours to bear then,*" he said. "*Keep it sheathed as often as you can. It is a strange and terrible thing, and there are many who seek such powers, in my world and yours. Just as it was stolen from its first master, so too may it be stolen again.*" The man glanced meaningfully at the trees. "*You will never know when wicked eyes may be watching.*"

Anna took the scabbard. She tied the grass belt around her waist, sliding the knife inside. The weapon hung easily by her waist, completely weightless.

"Thanks," she said.

The fairy-man smiled, but the smile was not a pleasant one.

"*I do you no great favors,*" he said. "*To see the people of the old wood is a curse. To know of our affairs is to invite us into your own lives, for good or ill. You may come to regret the decision you have made this day.*"

"Maybe," said Anna. "But thanks anyway."

Isabella gave the bear the second apple. It chomped enthusiastically at the rosy skin, juice dripping down its muzzle.

The fairy-man stood up, towering above the children. Anna hadn't realized how tall he was.

"Do not speak freely of the things you have seen," he said. His voice was darker now, closer to the twisting words he had whispered in the dungeon. *"You have chosen to court danger, but others have not. It is not your place to force the choice upon them."*

Max looked nervously at Anna. "We can tell Dad, though, can't we?"

Anna stared into the yellow eyes of the fairy. "No," she said. "I don't think we can."

The man nodded. Without saying another word, he turned and walked into the forest, his coat immediately camouflaged against the trunks of the trees. The bear jumped up as well. It gave Isabella's hand a brief lick, and then it too turned and ambled into the woods. In moments both the man and the bear had disappeared, lost in a haze of drifting leaves.

17

BEDTIME STORIES

THE PROFESSOR RETURNED TO THE INN just in time for dinner. He carried a huge stack of papers, each sheet covered in closely scribbled notes. His eyes were red and bloodshot, and his hair was a mess. Anna could tell just by looking at him that he'd barely slept since he left them the day before.

"It was fascinating," he said through a mouthful

of soup. "Absolutely fascinating. The history in these woods—well, it's astonishing just how much has happened."

"What did you find out?" asked Anna curiously.

"Well, there are some wonderful local legends," said the Professor. "There was a count who ruled over this area, and when he died the forest people burned down his castle. They thought he might return as a vampire, you see. Do you know anything about vampires?"

"Yes, I know a little bit," said Anna truthfully.

"Well, the whole story was ridiculous," said the Professor. "But the thing is, since the count died, people have been disappearing. Isn't that curious? It must just be the wolves, of course, but there are numerous records of people blaming the vampire. They call it the *strigoi* here. Do you know that word, Isabella?"

"Yes, I think I've heard it before," said Isabella.

"That's interesting," said the Professor. He smiled. "I wonder how much your grandmother knows about it all. She certainly puts a lot of garlic in this soup. Maybe it's to keep the vampires away!"

"Yes, that's probably why," said Max, raising his spoon to his lips. He dropped it back into his empty bowl—he had eaten every single mouthful of the peppery stew.

"You must have been hungry," said the Professor. "No vampires will be biting you tonight!"

The children laughed, though the Professor didn't understand why they found his joke so funny.

The Professor went to sleep early, excusing himself from the table and retiring to bed. The children gathered in Isabella's room, sitting in a circle on the floor.

"We're leaving tomorrow," said Anna sadly. "I wish you could come with us."

"Me too," said Isabella. "But Granny can't run the inn by herself. She needs me here to help her."

It didn't seem fair to Anna. The three friends had just shared an incredible adventure together. Why did they have to be split apart?

"We're not allowed to talk to anyone about what happened," said Anna. "That means only the three of us will ever know. It'll be like a secret club. So we need to stay in contact, just in case we ever need each other's help. Who knows what other spooky things might happen to us?"

"That gives me an idea," said Isabella. She walked over to her closet, taking out a handful of pens and a fresh new notebook with an emerald green cover. She selected a nice black pen and opened up the notebook, writing neatly across the top of the first page.

Anna looked over her shoulder, reading the words aloud.

"*The Vampire Knife.*"

"That's a good name," said Max.

"We have to write down the whole story," said Isabella. "Then we can send this journal back and forth between us, adding in any new things that we find out. That way we'll always know what the other members of the club are up to, and we'll be able to help with any problems they might have."

Anna was impressed. It wasn't as good as having Isabella with them all the time, but it was still a good idea.

For the next few hours, the children wrote down their story. Anna picked out some important pages from her fairy book (finally returned to her by Mrs. Dalca) that she would photocopy and paste into the journal when she got home. Isabella was excellent at drawing. She drew a picture of the vampire that was very close to how Anna and Max remembered it. Max found a picture of a cartoon vampire on one of his bubblegum cards, and they decided to stick the two pictures side by side to demonstrate the differences between the real monster and the fake one. They made a tracing of Max's hand, which was still very much dead, though none of the adults seemed to have noticed it. Anna wondered if they ever would.

Max was halfway through telling them what had happened as the vampire carried him up the mountain (a story Anna and Isabella had not heard yet) when Mrs. Dalca interrupted and insisted they go to sleep. Anna looked at the old woman closely, trying to imagine her as the little girl who met a wounded fairy in the woods. Mrs. Dalca had clearly made the decision to learn as little about the magical world as possible. Who had made the wiser decision—her, or them?

"I have something for you," rasped Mrs. Dalca

to Anna as she entered her bedroom. "It is to keep you warm on the coldest nights."

She held out something black and soft. Anna recognized it as the shadowy thing the old woman had been knitting with her fingers. She took it and stretched it out. It was a thick black scarf, identical to the one Isabella wore. Anna thought it might be the most beautiful piece of clothing she had ever owned.

"Thank you," she said. "It's wonderful. It's really wonderful."

Mrs. Dalca smiled at her.

"Good child," she said. "Now go to bed."

"How does the story end?" asked Max.

Anna barely heard him. She was busy looking out the car window, staring at all the trees that had been hidden by mist on their drive up the mountainside. They looked friendlier in the daytime, though she still wouldn't want to walk under them alone. It would have been fun to explore the woods with Isabella, following all of the trails on the old dusty map. Maybe there were even more fairies to find.

They had decided the white knife would stay with Anna. Isabella had assured them that the monster in her part of the world had been taken care of—with all of the Professor's work trips, the siblings would probably be the ones encountering a new danger. Max hadn't enjoyed that part of the conversation at all, but it made Anna excited. Her old red fairy book contained pages and pages detailing an entire menagerie of strange creatures, each with its own wicked motives and weird powers. Which other monsters were real? Anna patted the white knife by her waist, feeling a tinge of nervousness beneath her excitement. The blade had sat under the floorboards of the inn for years without anyone finding it. Would anybody really come looking for it now?

"How does the story end?" repeated Max.

Anna turned to look at her brother. The Professor had forgotten to build the barricade of suitcases between them, which meant the two children could talk normally for a change.

"I don't know what you mean," she said. "The story is over."

"Not the vampire story," said Max. "The story you were telling me before we got to the inn. The one where Max goes into the woods where the witch might live."

"Oh, right. That story," said Anna. "Give me a minute to think."

Max nodded contentedly. He scratched his head. Anna couldn't help but notice how horrible his pale fingers looked. She and Isabella may have accrued some interesting scars, but there was no denying Max had suffered the most of all.

"Okay," she said. "Max was creeping through the wood. He dropped his last breadcrumb and stood still in the middle of a clearing, wondering if he should go any farther without a trail to follow back. He didn't know that someone was creeping up behind him, their footsteps muffled by the rustling of the trees."

Max didn't look very scared. After what they had been through over the last two days, Anna doubted she'd ever be able to scare him again.

"Eventually Max felt something," she continued. "At first he thought it was just a breeze blowing on the back of his neck, but then he realized it was too warm to be the wind. Someone—or something— was breathing onto his skin. They were so close they could have touched him.

"And then a hand came down on Max's shoulder."

"Was it the witch?" asked Max.

Anna shook her head.

"Who was it?"

Anna paused for suspense. And then:

"It was Max's sister," she said. "She had seen Max playing close to the trees, and she knew that he might be taken by the wicked witch. So she had run into the woods after him, following the trail of breadcrumbs until she caught up to him in the clearing. Max was very glad to see her, and together they walked back out of the forest. And they reached home safely, and they lived happily ever after. The end."

"So nothing bad happened to Max?" asked Max. He seemed confused.

"Nope. Not a thing," said Anna.

"Oh," said Max.

The car wove along the mountain track. Eventually the rocky path would connect with a larger road, and then an even larger one, and then they would arrive at the airport and fly away to a whole new country. Anna didn't feel ready to leave Transylvania, but she couldn't help but feel excited. How long would it be before their next adventure? Where in the world would they end up next?

"I guess that was a good ending," said Max. "Can you tell me a new story now?"

Anna grinned.

THE END

Or is it the end?
Turn the page to find out where
Anna and Max are going next...

COMING SOON

THE TROLL HEART

After their adventures in Transylvania, Anna and Max just want to stay out of trouble—but trouble has other plans. The Professor is taking them to the cold and foggy fields of England, where a new mystery is already afoot. A small boy has vanished near a strange and mysterious river, lost without a trace.

Armed with her magical white knife, Anna is convinced that another monster is behind the boy's disappearance. But when the sinister secret of the river is finally revealed, will she and Max be able to save the missing boy—and themselves?

BE BOLD. BE BRAVE. BE TERRIFIED.

ACKNOWLEDGMENTS

A lot of very spooky people helped bring this story into the world. If you're curious enough, you can read their names here.

The good witches of Hardie Grant Egmont took words from my head and transformed them into a real book. They are masters of stories and ink, and it has been a privilege to work alongside them. My greatest thanks go to Marisa, Luna, Ilka, Haylee, Penelope, Annabel, and everyone else who helped bring this manuscript to life.

Ryan Andrews draws truly scary pictures; his illustrations of wolves, knives, and vampires are even spookier than the scenes I first imagined.

I also wish I could draw letters like Kristy Lund-White, who created all of the fiendish fonts found creeping across the front cover. For their wicked designs, I give them both my gratitude.

Adel Sarkozi comes from the land of vampires and was an invaluable asset in reviewing my use of the Romanian language. *Mulțumesc!*

This story was written in 2015, during the coldest winter that Melbourne has experienced in my lifetime. Thanks go to my housemates, Amelia and Daniel, who always looked after me on those freezing nights, and to all the other friends who came and played games with us until the witching hour: Corey, Marcus, Eliza, Tom, Robert, Laura, Patrick, Ava, Jacqui, Matthew, and Emily (to name just a few).

Finally, I acknowledge my family, who have read to me, encouraged me, and terrified me for twenty-five spooky years. Thanks go to my parents, Teresa and Phil; my sister, Kit; my uncles and aunties, Danny and Beth, Jacqueline and Karl, Peter and Di, and Shane and JR; my cousins, Patrick, Harry, Gypsy, Jesse, and Raffy; and to my grandfather, Kenny. Further thanks go to my girlfriend, Jemima, and to *her* parents, Ruth and Frank. Mt. Rowan may be infested with witches, but it's a much safer place with all of you around.

ABOUT THE AUTHOR

JACK HENSELEIT was born on a winter evening in 1991, just after the stroke of midnight. When the weather is dark and stormy, he writes fairy tales—*real* fairy tales, where witches and goblins play tricks on unwary girls and boys. Not all of the tales have happy endings.

The Witching Hours: The Vampire Knife is his first novel. Visit jackhenseleit.com to learn more about Jack.

THE CHIANGS OF CHINA

By ELMER T. CLARK

The
CHIANGS
of CHINA

ABINGDON-COKESBURY PRESS
New York   Nashville

THE CHIANGS OF CHINA
COPYRIGHT, MCMXLIII
BY WHITMORE & STONE

WAR EDITION

Complete text. Reduced size in compliance
with orders of the War Production Board
for conserving paper and other materials.

SET UP, PRINTED, AND BOUND BY THE
PARTHENON PRESS AT NASHVILLE, TEN-
NESSEE, UNITED STATES OF AMERICA

GENERALISSIMO AND MADAME CHIANG KAI-SHEK

At Hankow in 1938, not long before the Japanese advance
forced removal of the capital further west

Foreword

THIS little book is a human-interest story about one of the world's most famous groups of people. The saga of the Soong family and its connections—the Suns, the Kungs, and especially the Chiangs—has thrilled the imagination of millions. Here are romance and adventure, revolution and intrigue, the crash of empire and the birth of a nation, the rise from poverty and obscurity to the dizziest heights of power and glory. All the elements for the making of a thriller are here. If it were fiction instead of solid fact, if touched by the imagination of a novelist rather than the reporter's steady adherence to the record, the romance of this amazing family would rival the most popular adventure story of all literature.

Although the author cannot qualify as an old China hand, or claim any unusual degree of authority in the field, he nevertheless accepted readily the suggestion to tell in simple fashion the story of these notable careers. For many years documents, stories, articles, and pictures relating to this family have been passing through his editorial hands; and these, together with the well-known books and other literature on the subject listed in the Bibliography, constitute the source materials. Some are primary, but more are secondary in nature. Much—very much—has been omitted, but nothing has been put in that is not substantiated by the records. It is a true story.

It is hoped that none will expect this little volume to be what it is not, or to do what it does not undertake. It is not a history, not a dissertation, not a biography. Nor is it addressed to authorities or research specialists. It is a piece of reporting about some great and good people and the influences that made them what they are, addressed to those Americans who are interested in the creative influences quite as much as in the people themselves.

The author is especially indebted to Dr. Y. C. Yang, president of Soochow University, visiting professor at Bowdoin College, and staff member of the Chinese Government's News Service in New York City, for his invaluable and careful criticism and advice.

Elmer T. Clark

Contents

Illustrations

1

Charles Jones Soon in America

A MONG the craft in the harbor of Wilmington, North Carolina, in November of 1880 lay a cutter of the service now known as the United States Coast Guard. Its being there was nothing unusual, but this time Destiny was aboard it in the person of a boy named Soon Chiao-chun (or Yao-ju). Already at fourteen years of age his career had a touch of adventure, prophecy of the almost fabulous future that lay before him.

It seems that the boy was born in the village of Weichan, or Kuisan, on Hainan Island, off the south coast of Kwangtung province in China, in 1866. The family had been Shansi people, but in an early day they had fled the civil wars in that region and become shippers in South China. In due course they followed the custom of the Cantonese and sent out members of the family to establish shops at various places along the eastern seaboard of the United States. When only nine years old the little Chiao-chun was sent with a brother to East India, though why they went and what they did there are among undiscovered facts. At any rate, he turned up three years later, in 1878, as an apprentice in his uncle's tea and silk shop in Boston, having left his brother in East India.

He was really more than an apprentice. As the uncle was sonless and had no one to perform the ancestral rites at the family tombs, which could be performed only by males, he adopted Chiao-chun and gave the boy his own name—a prac-

13

tice more or less customary among families without sons in China. The lad was to learn the tea and silk business and eventually become a merchant on his own.

But young Soon had no taste for merchandising—so he told his children later—and his disinclination turned into positive aversion when two Chinese students dropped in and pointed out the glories of an American education and the favored position to be enjoyed in the old country by foreign-trained citizens. Soon was to meet both of them later and to be again profoundly influenced by them. They were Wan Bing-chung and New Shan-chow, cousins, who were members of the Chinese Educational Commission brought to this country by Dr. Yung Wing, a Yale graduate. Listening to these students, Soon conceived new ambitions, and when they were frowned on by his uncle he promptly ran away and joined the Coast Guard.

By one of the mysterious ways in which God is said to work in performing His wonders, it turned out that one of the boy's officers was a deeply religious man, who listened to young Soon's story and sympathized with his ambition. He treated the boy kindly, probably connived a little in keeping the uncle in ignorance of the adopted son's whereabouts when the vessel was in Boston waters, and at convenient times explained the Christian religion and gently exhorted the youngster to exercise saving faith in Jesus Christ. The seed fell upon good ground.

This man, if not a member, at least was a regular attendant of the Fifth Street Methodist Church in Wilmington when his ship was in that port and enjoyed friendships among the members. When he dropped anchor there on or about the first of November, he looked up Colonel Roger Moore and Mrs. Tom Ramsey and related the story of the Chinese boy whom he had almost persuaded to be a Christian. Methodists in that part of the world then regarded with considerable seriousness their duty to the "heathen"—especially the Chinese variety, for China was their main mission field—and here, in the person of what was probably the only Chinese ever seen in Wilmington up to that time, was an opportunity and challenge dropped by providence upon their very doorsteps. They accepted it, and thereby started a movement in China which continues to have momentous results.

The Rev. Thomas Page Ricaud was pastor of the Fifth Street Church at the time. This good man was a leading minister of tidewater North Carolina, and something of a Horatio Alger hero in his own right. Orphaned in Baltimore at an early age, he was adopted by relatives and taken to Mexico. He studied for the Roman Catholic priesthood at the University of Mexico, fought as a revolutionist, was wounded and captured in one of the many civil wars, went to France, returned to America, and took up the study of law in Virginia. He was converted in a revival and became a preacher in Virginia in 1841, later transferring to North Carolina.

When Soon came to Wilmington, this pastor was conducting a revival meeting, and friends took the boy to the services. The preaching stimulated the work of grace already begun by the good sailor, and a few nights later he went forward with others and knelt at the altar of the church as a penitent in the current fashion. One who was present reported that "he seemed quite happy and his face was shining" when he arose from his knees. He returned to the Ramsey home, shook hands with the group of church people who joyfully accompanied the new convert, told each one how he had "found the Saviour," and declared he wanted to go back to China and tell his people about Christ. There has never been any reasonable doubt about the genuineness of Soon's conversion, since his whole later life and the record of his family are living witnesses.

He joined the Fifth Street Church the following Sunday. It was something of an event in Wilmington. The Sunday *Star,* November 7, 1880, announced that candidates would be baptized at the church that morning. "A Chinese convert," ran the story, "will be one of the subjects of the solemn rite, being probably the first Celestial that has ever submitted to the ordinance of baptism in North Carolina." And on the following Tuesday the same newspaper said, "The service at the Fifth Street Methodist Episcopal Church, South, on Sunday morning last, in connection with the baptism of the Chinese youth alluded to in our last, is said to have been exceedingly impressive."

When Mr. Ricaud laid his hands on the head of Soon Chiao-chun the young man took the baptismal name of Charles Jones Soon. For more than half a century it has been said that Charles Jones was the name of the friendly officer on the revenue cutter and that the adoption of the cognomen was Soon's way of honoring him. But the tradition has been shaken by the Coast Guard authorities, who declare there was no such man in the service at that time.[1] Anyway, he became Charles Jones Soon and made the name famous. Probably anybody who undertook to Americanize Chiao-chun would turn it out as Charles Jones.

---

[1] The oft-repeated tradition is that Charles Jones was boatswain—some say skipper—of the cutter "Schuyler Colfax" and that Soon reached Wilmington as a member of her crew. But Coast Guard officials say no Charles Jones was in the service during any of the years concerned, and nobody of that name was ever on the "Colfax," as is proved by the muster rolls for every year of her existence. They further declare that Soon did not come to Wilmington on the "Colfax" but rather was on another cutter first, made his way privately to Wilmington, and there shipped aboard the "Colfax" for a brief time. On the other hand, persons still living in Wilmington claim they knew Charles Jones; and Mr. Ricaud's daughter,

Courtesy Fifth Ave. Meth. Church, Wilmington, N. C.

A picture snatched from the flames

THE ALTAR WHERE SOON WAS BAPTIZED

Interior of the old Fifth Street Church, Wilmington, North Carolina

THE REV. THOMAS PAGE RICAUD

GENERAL JULIAN S. CARR

His conversion and baptism gave a new trend to Soon's career. His thoughts turned to religious work and an eventual return to China as a missionary, and the thoughts of the church at Wilmington turned in the same direction. But he had enlisted in the government service, and the newly made plans were all contingent on securing his release. This was accomplished through the instrumentality of Colonel Moore, who seems to have been a man of some influence in the necessary circles.

Soon remained in Wilmington several months, probably under the care and tutelage of Mr. Ricaud. At one Sunday afternoon meeting at the church he gave a "thrilling testimony," expressing gratitude to the members of the church for their kindness to a stranger and declaring that he wanted to secure an education and return to China as a missionary. "The idea of sending a saved heathen back out among the heathens appealed strongly to the good church people," says James Burke.[2] The pastor sought out General Julian S. Carr at Durham. General Carr was a Confederate veteran, a rich manufacturer, and a devoted church member interested in all good causes, and he saw the missionary implications involved. So Soon went to the Carr home in Durham, where he was on trial and inspection for a period while the General decided whether the young man was worth an investment. He was;

who still lives in Wilmington, declares her father suggested to Soon adopting Jones's name. C. D. Barclift, present pastor of the Fifth Avenue Methodist Church at Wilmington—successor to the Fifth Street Church—who wrote a dissertation at Duke University on the subject, declares, in spite of the Coast Guard's assertion, "I have indisputable proof that Soong did come into the port of Wilmington on the 'Colfax' " He further quotes J. T. Hawkins, long-time resident of Wilmington, to the effect that Jones was boatswain on the "Colfax." The author has a photostatic copy of a letter written by Soon on board the "Colfax" at Wilmington on January 14, 1881.

[2] *My Father in China* (New York: Farrar & Rinehart, 1942), p. 7.

and in April, 1881, he entered Trinity College, now Duke University, as the protégé of the philanthropist, whom he began to call "Father Carr," and of the Sunday school he attended during his stay in Durham.

He at once transferred his membership from Wilmington to the congregation at Trinity, in Randolph County near High Point, where the college was then located. Dr. Braxton Craven was pastor of the church, which worshiped in the college chapel, as well as president of Trinity College; and when he received Charles Jones Soon into membership he appropriately preached on, "Go ye into all the world, and preach the gospel to every creature."

Under date of June 9, 1881, President Craven reported to the board of trustees: "At our last conference, Rev. T. Page Ricaud made a proposition to me to take a Chinese boy, then at Wilmington. Complete arrangements were made, and he arrived here some two months ago. . . . . The Durham Sunday School pays his board and the college gives the rest." He was listed in the catalogue as Charles J. Soon, Weichan, China, under "Special and Preparatory Students." He certainly was not prepared to enter the college in any other category.

Soon lived at Trinity in the home of Professor W. T. Gannaway, but studied in the home of President Craven, with Mrs. Craven as his "devoted friend and competent tutor." While in the Coast Guard service he had learned to make hammocks, and at Durham and during the summer holidays he supported himself by selling these. He remained in Trinity one full scholastic year plus the weeks between his entrance in April and the June commencement. The exact nature of his studies is not recorded, but it has been supposed that he did some real college work during the last months. At any rate, he made a satisfactory record, for he was able to enter the graduate Biblical Department at Vanderbilt University the following year. But academic standards were more adaptable to human needs in the eighties than they are today.

On June 25, 1881, young Soon wrote a letter to his father and told the story of his conversion. He wrote it in English, but it was the type of English used by a neophyte in the use of the language. He told his father that he had "found Christ our Saviour," and that he was being educated "so I can go back to China and tell you about the kindness of the friends in Durham and the grace of God."

I remember [he continued] when I was a little boy you took me to a great temple to worshipped the wooden Gods. . . . . if you do worships all your life time would not do a bit goods. in our old times they know nothing about Christ. but now I had found a Saviour he is comforted me where ever I go to. please let your ears be open so you can hear what the spirit say and your eyes looks up so you may see the glory of God.

This letter he sent to Dr. Young J. Allen, superintendent of the Southern Methodist Mission in Shanghai, with the request that it be forwarded to his father. But the missive was never delivered. Dr. Allen could not locate the family in South China.

All, including Soon himself, were agreed that the young Chinese convert should study theology and go back to preach the gospel to his own people. So in the fall of 1882 he gave Mrs. Craven one of his hammocks, kissed her good-by with deep and tearful emotion, and departed to enter the theological seminary at Vanderbilt University in Nashville. Vanderbilt at the time was a Southern Methodist institution and the training ground for preachers of that faith and order. The Biblical Department was housed in Wesley Hall—the original building of this name, destroyed by fire in 1932—an imposing edifice in the architecture of that period, with "Schola Prophetarum" over the door; and there the young Chinese theologue lived, studied, and worshiped with other budding preachers from the various Southern states.

Contemporary accounts indicate that he was contented, jovial, happy, and almost universally popular, but he experienced occasional homesickness for China and the dear friends who coddled him at Durham. One of his classmates, the Rev. John C. Orr, reports:

At first the boys paid little or no attention to Soon. He was more of a curiosity than anything else. He was just a Chinaman. But this soon changed. He fell into the classes of the writer, and they became not only well acquainted, but intimate friends. He had a fine mind, soon learned to use the English language with accuracy and fluency, and was usually bubbling over with wit and humor and good nature. The boys soon became fond of him, and took him into all the social activities of the campus. His handwriting was like a copy-plate, with the hairline touch and the shading flourishes. He wrote the visiting cards for the boys. Although somewhat handicapped on account of his ignorance of the English language, he prepared his lessons well, passed all his examinations, and graduated with honor in his class of four in Theology.

It was the custom of some of the more zealous of the boys to meet in the little chapel of Wesley Hall before breakfast on Sunday mornings for a sort of experience meeting. They would sing and pray and tell their religious experience. One morning Soon (as we called him) got up and stood awhile before he said anything. Then his lips trembled and he said: "I feel so little. I get so lonesome. So far from my people. So long among strangers. I feel just like I was a little chip floating down the Mississippi River. But I know that Jesus is my Friend, my Comforter, my Savior." The tears were running down his cheeks, and before he could say anything more a dozen of the boys were around him,

with their arms about him, and assuring him that they loved him
as a brother. Soon broke up the meeting that morning.[3]

The Rev. Daniel H. Tuttle, another fellow student, became
pastor of the Fifth Street Church in Wilmington in December,
1884. Soon visited the scene of his conversion after his graduation from Vanderbilt and received a Bible as a gift from
the congregation. Mr. Tuttle declared that the people regarded him as "their son in the gospel" and that he preached
two or three times "to the spiritual edification of all who
heard him."

"I have been preaching some," Soon said at a farewell service arranged by Dean Tillett, the "grand old man" at Vanderbilt, "and I have found pleasure and joy in preaching the
Gospel of Christ. I go back to my people in China, to preach
the Gospel of Christ to them, and to live the life of Christ
among them."

During the summers young Soon sold his hammocks and
books and frequently preached and held revival meetings.
One favorite spot for him was the hospitable home of Mr.
and Mrs. J. E. Stockard, near Franklin, Tennessee. There
was an attractive niece, Sally—later Mrs. J. M. Fly—to whom
the boy gave his photograph; she was teased about it and
threw the picture in the fire, but it was rescued by her mother
and is still preserved. But he kept in touch with his Durham
friends and during the vacations spent his time with "Father
Carr" when he was not on the road selling books and hammocks. He was especially attached to Miss Annie Southgate,
daughter of a Durham businessman, and once declared in a
letter, "I love you more than anyone in America." Writing
to her from Washington, D. C., however, he confessed that
he had "fallen in love with Miss Bell," and added, "Don't you

[3] "Recollections of Charlie Soon," *World Outlook*, April, 1938, p. 140.

think that is too bad, for I have to leave my heart in Washington and I go to China." When Miss Southgate died, after Soon had returned to China, he wrote her father an interesting letter of condolence:

It is a matter of great sorrow to learn of the death of Miss Annie, though on the contrary do rejoice to know that she is happier in heaven than could possibly be on earth. And no doubt all these work for good to them that love God. May God comfort you all and sustain you with His tender love and grace and finally when our work is done in this life we may all meet her on that happy shore where there is no parting.

Miss Annie was one of my best friends. Her Christian example is worthy of attention. When I left America I had no idea of such event would have occurred so soon and that we are not permitted to meet again on this side of Jordan. O this is sad to think of the sweetest flower God has plucked off and took away from us; but that very identical flower is blooming in the garden of God in heaven. Happy art thou who sleeps in the Lord. And thrice happy art thou who being translated from earthly sorrow to heavenly joy. May God keep us from sin and weakness and finally translate us to His home where we will meet all our friends and loved ones and to live with Christ forever.

Soon graduated in theology at Vanderbilt in the spring of 1885. He received a diploma but not a degree because he was not a college graduate. He wanted to take up the study of medicine to fit himself better for service in China, and General Carr was willing to finance him; but Bishop Holland N. McTyeire, chancellor of Vanderbilt and also in charge of the Mission in China, refused to hear of it, for reasons that will appear. So he applied for admission to the North Carolina Annual Conference of the Methodist Episcopal Church, South. The conference, meeting at Charlotte, November 25–December 2, 1885, by special request of Bishop McTyeire took the extraordinary action of admitting Charles Jones **Soon** "on trial" and at the same session, without waiting for the results of the usual two-year trial period, ordaining him and appointing him as a missionary to China.

There had never been any doubt that he was to do missionary work among his own people in China. That desire he expressed on the very night of his conversion, and he repeated it on other occasions. The missionary urge—the unique strategy of sending a converted "heathen" back to preach the gospel to his countrymen—was the motive which prompted the churches at Wilmington and Durham, General Carr, Dr. Craven, and all the others who aided him. Bishop McTyeire understood it so, and was eager to send him on his way as soon as possible. The bishop wrote Dr. Allen this unique and suggestive letter about the case:

VANDERBILT UNIVERSITY
NASHVILLE, TENNESSEE
July 8, 1885

MY DEAR DOCTOR ALLEN:

We expect to send *Soon* out to you this fall, with Dr. Park. I trust you will put him, at once, to *circuit work,* walking if not riding. *Soon* wished to stay a year or two longer to study medicine to be equipped for higher usefulness, etc. And his generous patron, Mr. Julian Carr, was not unwilling to continue helping.

But we thought better that the *Chinaman* that is in him should not all be worked out before he labors among the Chinese. Already he has "felt the easy chair"—and is not averse to the comforts of higher civilization. No fault of his.

Let our young man, on whom we have bestowed labor, begin to *labor.* Throw him into the ranks: *no side place.* His desire to study medicine was met by the information that we have already as many *doctors* as the Mission needed, and one more.

I have good hope that, with your judicious handling, our *Soon*

may do well. It will greatly encourage similar work here if he does. The destinies of many are bound up in his case. . . . .

Yr. bro. in Christ,

H. N. McTyeire

Thus bustled off before the comforts of higher civilization could complete their evil work upon him, Soon sailed back to China. He left in December, 1885, soon after his ordination and appointment, traveling with Dr. W. H. Park, who was destined to become outstanding as a medical missionary. They reached Shanghai in January, and Soon entered into the work of the mission. He was not to be a great missionary, as such, for his superiors already had a mind-set toward him that could not have been overcome. But his influence will remain long after the deans of the China mission have been forgotten.

2

Charles Jones Soong in China

B<small>ACK</small> in China, Soon added a g to his name and prepared to become a pastor. After living for a short period with Dr. Park at Soochow, he moved in with a native preacher to study the Shanghai dialect, which was so different from that of South China that he must all but master a new language. This preacher was Dzau Tsz-zeh, better and widely known as Charlie Marshall—an interesting character who spoke English with a heavy Southern accent from serving in the American Civil War as attendant to Confederate Colonel D. C. Kelley, an early missionary to China. Soong had much to learn also about the customs of the country, for he had been away from China since boyhood. On one occasion in the good American manner he tried to call on a young teacher in one of the Mission's schools, not taking account of the Chinese method of courtship only through the parents—the young people should not see each other until their wedding day. The principal was so scandalized that she locked the girl in her room until Soong left town.

When the China Mission Conference was organized and held its first session in November, 1886, Soong became one of its original members—"on trial" but already ordained—and was appointed to the Kwen-san circuit in the Soochow district. He set to work with energy at his new post, no less eager than on the day of his conversion to preach the gospel to his own people; but he found difficulties neither he nor the American friends who had so enthusiastically encouraged him had ever imagined. Although to his superiors and other foreigners he was a "native," to his own people he was practically a foreigner. He was an utter stranger, his family being far to the south, was still only partially familiar with the language and the customs, and in all his attitudes was indeed more American than Chinese. James Burke relates that when his large father and the small Soong appeared together at Kwen-san a countryman remarked loudly, "Two foreign devils. A giant and a dwarf." [1]

But Soong had abundant faith and zeal. Something of his spirit is revealed in letters to his friends in America during the following months. In his letter to J. H. Southgate in connection with the death of Miss Annie, written from Kwen-san on February 4, 1887, he reported:

I have begun to preach in this dialect, though not as fluently as I would like. . . . . Kuensan [Kwen-san] is a walled city of four miles in circumference. It has a population of 300,000, including the suburbs. At present we have three different denominations represented here, besides the various sects of the heathen religions: we, the Southern Methodists, the Southern Baptists, the French Catholic, the Buddhist, the Taoist and the Mohammedan. . . . . Please pray for me and my work. May God give us abundance of success in the coming year, and that we may experience more deeply of His love to us-ward.

That some of the difficulties were being overcome by experience is suggested by the more optimistic tone of a letter written after over a year at Kwen-san to the *Raleigh Christian Advocate*. The date is December 21, 1887.

The outlook is very promising. The Spirit of the Lord is rapid-

---

[1] *My Father in China*, p. 51.

ly making His way into the hearts of His benighted people......
Our China Mission Conference has met and closed......I returned
to Kuensan for another year. By the grace and help of God, I
hope to do better and more work for my Saviour than ever I did
before......

But perhaps the promising outlook was due to another fac-
tor, about which Soong had written Mr. Southgate not long
before: "I must tell you I am different from what I used to
be. I am married. The ceremony was performed by Rev.
C. F. Reid, of our Mission." And thereby hangs a tale.

Romance cropped up at Kwen-san when Soong encountered
S. C. New, one of the Chinese students he had met in Boston.
In view of the young preacher's loneliness in the parsonage,
New suggested marriage, and proposed his own wife's nine-
teen-year-old sister, Miss Ni Kwei-tseng, as the prospective
bride. He even went so far as to offer personally to fulfill the
functions of the go-between necessitated by Chinese ethics,
since of course the suitor could not hope to see Kwei-tseng until the wedding day. There were three Ni girls and the third
had been or was soon to be married to B. C. Wan, the other
old Boston student friend. There was but one drawback—
Kwei-tseng had "big" feet. The feverish reaction to the bind-
ings placed on her feet in babyhood had been so serious that
they had had to be left off. This was no drawback at all in
the Soong opinion, since all American girls had "big" feet,
and he had no taste for the crushed and misshapen stumps
produced by the Chinese foot-binding custom. Soong was
enthusiastic. All worked out as the friends had plotted, and
Soong married Miss Ni.

Miss Ni was a girl of superior quality sprung from a long
line of important Christian ancestors. She was directly descended from Zi Kwang-kyi (or Hsu Kwang-chi), a prime

minister of one of the Ming emperors, who was converted by
Roman Catholic missionaries in 1601. The family lived on
the Zi estate in a Shanghai suburb as good Catholics until
Kwei-tseng's mother married Mr. Ni, the family tutor and a
scholar who had been converted by missionaries of the London Missionary Society and had become an Episcopalian.

Madame Soong's family history has many tales of high interest in Chinese circles, including one, related by her to W. B.
Burke and recorded by his son, concerning the loss of the
family pearls by Mother Ni as she hobbled away on her "little"
feet before the approach of the Taiping rebels in 1850. The
pearls were priceless family possessions, taken from the cere-
monial coat and headdress of a Ming emperor and presented
to Candida—as she was called by Europeans—a daughter of
Zi Kwang-kyi. Candida was the Roman Catholic enthusiast
who built churches and hospitals all over the place and finally taught Bible tales to all the blind storytellers of Peking and
sent them out as unwitting evangelists.[2]

The marriage of the Soongs turned out to be a genuine love
match. She joined his church and accepted its holiness traditions as well as its puritan morality. Among all Chinese
who knew and cared about such things her piety, good works,
careful training of her children, and general influence were
known; and as time goes on her character and memory become more and more legendary. On her death in 1931 the
children, following the Chinese custom, sent out a biography,
which Emily Hahn quotes as follows:

She was the second daughter of our maternal grandfather,
Yuin San; his native town was originally Yuyiao [near Ningpo,
in Chekiang Province]. He was a scholar and well learned in
law. He was a political adviser, which work took him to Chuan
Sha; there he settled down and thereafter lived with his family.

---

[2] *My Father in China*, pp. 52-53.

Our maternal grandmother was of the Hsu family, which is very well known in the west part of Shanghai. [The district of "Sikawei" was named after the family; literally, "Hsu's corner."] There has been a Hsu in official life in an unbroken line since the illustrious Wen Ting-kung [Hsu Kwang-ki] down to Fu Yuin, our maternal great-grandfather, who was of the sixteenth generation of Wen Ting-kung's descendants. He was a commander of the army that protected the districts, and fought at Shanghai, Paoshan, Nan Wei and Chuan Sha, where he was killed in battle. In admiration of his courage and his accomplishments the authorities built a temple dedicated to his honor at his birthplace, and up until today the inhabitants have never stopped paying tribute to him.

Ever since the end of the Ming Dynasty, after Wen Ting-kung was converted to Christianity and began to respect the new education, the family has maintained this tradition, treating their children in a manner absolutely free of sex prejudice. Our maternal grandmother and our mother were baptized Protestants when they were children, and faithfully obeyed the Ten Commandments. Our mother was very clever and was her parents' favorite. When she was only three or four years old she began her studies under a private tutor: she entered school at the age of eight; at fourteen, she was promoted to the Pei Wan Girls' High School at the West Gate and was graduated at seventeen. She was particularly good in mathematics, and she loved the piano. At eighteen she was married to our father, Yao-ju. They gave birth to us six children: Eling, Chingling, Tseven, Mayling, Tse-liang, Tsean. . . . .

Our mother looked after the domestic affairs and managed to make both ends meet. . . . . She also helped the poor and was a patron of schools and churches.

Although our parents were not very well off, yet she helped us all to live in happiness and comfort, and this she kept up through the most difficult times. . . . .[3]

---

[3] *The Soong Sisters* (New York: Doubleday, Doran & Co., 1941), pp. 22-23.

With this excellent helpmeet to comfort and encourage him, Soong completed successfully his trial period and at the Conference of 1888 was received into full connection as a "traveling" preacher—as ministers in the Methodist itinerancy system have been called since the horseback days of John Wesley. He was reappointed to Kwen-san for a third year and in 1889 was sent to the T'sih-pao circuit in the Shanghai district. Then at the Conference held in October, 1890, there was written in the minutes this significant item: "Q.16. Who are located this year? C. J. Soon, at his own request." Translated from the Methodist, this means that he ceased to "travel" and became a local preacher.

Soong was not giving up pastoral work entirely; the Conference appointed him to Tse So in the Shanghai district as a "supply"—a local preacher filling a vacancy but not necessarily devoting full time to it. But he proceeded to go into business also as an agent for the American Bible Society. The change is not to be taken as indicating the cooling of his evangelistic ardor nor the abandonment of his ambition to tell his people of Christ, but rather as an adjustment to a method more suited to his character and abilities. From the vantage point of later years there seems something providential about it; but even then Soong was justified in feeling that he was still a missionary, that he was serving the Christian cause in general and the Methodist Mission in particular no less by making Chinese Bibles available than by being a pastor.

Nevertheless, certain unpleasant circumstances conected with his work for the Mission had a part in the shift, and it was not made without regrets. No doubt there were some pangs of conscience too when he remembered the career his American friends had planned for him. In a letter dated October 19, 1892, he explained to them through the columns of the *Raleigh Christian Advocate*:

My reason for leaving the Mission was it did not give me sufficient to live upon. I could not support myself, wife and children, with about $15.00 of U. S. money per month. I hope that my friends will understand that my leaving the Mission does not mean the giving up of preaching Christ and Him crucified. At present I am connected with the American Bible Society, but I am still doing my own work connected with our Church. My laborers in the field, Brothers Hill and Bonnell, will bear testimony to this. So my leaving the Mission simply means that I am an independent worker of our Methodist Mission, or one who tries to do as much as he can for the Mission, without depending on the Church at home for his support.

I am now in charge of our New Methodist Church, which is the gift of Brother Moore, of Kansas City, U. S. A., and which is the finest native church in the city. We have a very large Sunday School in this Church, and a fine staff of teachers. I have a nice Sunday School class, which is composed of young men and old.

Some of the readers of this letter were undoubtedly surprised at the low salary reported by Soong. They had ordained him a member of their Conference and appointed him a missionary to China; a missionary should be better paid than this. But they had not realized what a problem they were creating, though a like situation has been a headache to many a missionary administrator. Soong's American training and the ability he was later to demonstrate entitled him to the salary and status of a missionary, and his having "felt the easy chair" made him desire them. But the missionary authorities expected him to be a "native preacher." He was a Chinese, and to grant him the pay and standing of a missionary might create jealousies in the ranks.

Even before he had seen the recruit, the superintendent, Dr. Young J. Allen, had made up his mind on the subject and was plainly worried about the complications he knew would result. He wrote to the Board of Missions at Nashville inquiring about "the salary of Mr. Soon" and "how the Board expects to treat him." He wanted to know about his "status and pay" because "there is much that is embarrassing in this case." He said there were boys in his Anglo-Chinese College in Shanghai who were "far his superiors" because they knew Chinese as well as English and had done "composition and translation that has won the encomiums of our eldest and ablest missionaries." "Composition and translation" meant more than preaching ability to Dr. Allen, who was concerned because young Soong would never become "a Chinese scholar," and spoke of paying him "far beyond his deserts" even before learning what his deserts actually were.

Now Dr. Allen was one of the great missionaries of the world, and he laid the foundation of what became one of the most excellent missions anywhere. He was a scholar who preferred the long view and the thorough method. He mastered the Chinese language and culture, translated a literature, and founded schools which made contributions of incalculable worth. But his passion for education made him discount direct preaching. Men said that he never invited the "native preachers" to his home but associated exclusively with scholars among the Chinese. It was plain from the beginning that Soong was not to find in Dr. Allen the same kind of sympathy he had encountered in Durham. Indeed, there was a clash upon his arrival when the superintendent refused to let him visit his father, whom he had not seen since boyhood. He mentioned this with some bitterness in a letter to Mr. Southgate, declaring he would ask to be transferred to Japan rather than work under Dr. Allen.

Being "located," then, Soong established himself in Shanghai and became a good businessman. Within a few years he

MADAME KWEI-TSENG NI SOONG

CHARLES JONES SOONG IN 1886

During a stopover in Yokohama on his voyage to Shanghai to become a missionary. The costume is Japanese

founded a printing house of his own and began publishing Bibles, which were distributed far and wide through the trade and by colporteurs and all the missions. Wealthy friends built a flour mill in the city and, recognizing the value of Soong's American experience and forthright manner, asked him to become the manager, a post he held the rest of his life. In a modest way he became something of an industrialist and was the first agent to import foreign machinery. His profits from the various enterprises were satisfactory, and the erstwhile circuit preacher became a prosperous man, even a rich man according to the prevalent standards.

He built a house in Hongkew, so far "out in the country" that many friends feared too much Americanism had mildly deranged the man; but as in the case of American suburbs the city in the course of time encroached and packed closely about it. The family owns it now, or did own it until the Japanese came in 1937. It was such a house as a circuit rider could never aspire to, and to the Chinese it had Soong eccentricities all over it. The architecture was Sino-American, and so were the furnishings: green and yellow bathtubs with dragons on them, comfortable beds with American mattresses, a piano, upholstered chairs and sofa, gas radiators, and other refinements which justified Bishop McTyeire's dread that Soong was "not averse to the comforts of higher civilization." There was a stream in front, a well-enclosed courtyard, a dozen rooms inside, and a servant's house with kitchen and storerooms in the rear. He lived in a style which won the approval of his friends—but he scandalized them by working in his garden.

Charles Jones Soong had come up in the world. He was a respected and affluent businessman, an educated man and a teacher, consulted and honored and asked to participate in the social and economic life about him. But in his own mind Soong was a missionary still. He retained his status as an ordained minister and often exercised the functions thereof. He regarded his Bible printing press as a missionary institution, the publishing house of the Christian mission in China. He was a leader in organizing the Y. M. C. A., and in nearly everything else that looked to the conversion of his people and the Christianization of the nation. And in their home the Soongs lived the part.

He also became a revolutionist. Now the Revolution was long overdue in China, and Soong no doubt regarded the creation of a better order as a part of the social mission of Christianity. The forward-looking missionaries thought so too. Dr. Sun Yat-sen, the leader of the revolutionary movement, was a Christian, and this probably commended the man and his highly idealistic plans to Soong. So he attached himself to the Sun enterprise.

Sun Yat-sen is today all but a god in China. His body rests in a million-dollar shrine; his picture hangs in the schools, and before it the pupils make salutes; his brief Last Will and Testament, which bequeathed nothing save hopes and aspirations, is repeated as a sort of creed in Nationalist circles. But it was not always thus; it did not become so until he died —as has been true of many prophets. In life he was an idealistic dreamer, impractical and somewhat visionary, steadfast in pursuit of his political aims, but with respect to other convictions swept hither and yon by many appealing doctrines; it was said that he espoused Christianity, atheism, democracy, communism, foreignism, and anti-foreignism at various times. Nevertheless, he is properly regarded as the George Washington of modern China and father of the republic.

Sun was born in 1867. His father was a Christian—some said he was a preacher—and the boy was sent to a church school in Honolulu, where his brother had preceded him. There he imbibed the modern ideals of equality and democracy prevalent in Western nations, and when he returned to China he was full of passion for these notions and set about preaching them with the fervor of all youthful idealists. He directed especial vituperation at the Manchu government and the ruling dynasty. On one occasion he broke a finger from a great wooden image of the emperor, crying out to the people, "Now you see what sort of a god you have to protect your village; I break and twist his finger off, and he holds the same grin as before." He had to flee to Hong Kong, where he studied medicine and became the first modern medical graduate in China.

About the time Charlie Soong first met him, he organized a secret radical society called Hsingchunghui—literally the Society for the Regeneration of China, or the Advance-China Society. Later this and various other groups were merged into the Tungmenghui—the Get-Together Society or Dare-to-Dies—with branches throughout the world preparing for the Revolution. As it developed, its platform became the overthrow of the Manchu throne, establishment of democracy and a republic, elimination of foreign control, uplift of women and the laboring classes, and development of the nearly unlimited resources of the country. All this was set down in Sun's famous "San Min Chu I"—"Three Principles of the People"—the political platform of the Kuomintang, the nationalist party which grew out of the Tungmenghui. This party had four planks and a reasonable and progressive plan for carrying them out: to overthrow the Manchus, regain China for the Chinese, establish a republic, and equalize land ownership.

The prosperous preacher-merchant, Soong, entered into all this hand and glove. It was not long before Dr. Sun was in and out of the Soong house constantly when he was in China, and he lived with the Soongs after the movement began to succeed. The early, undercover meetings of the conspirators were held in Soong's house, and Soong had a hand in sponsoring the midnight meetings in Chang's Garden, which became more and more open as the prospects for success increased. Most important of all, Soong's presses turned out the tracts and pamphlets which flooded China with the doctrines of the Revolution.

All this was surreptitious, of course. Even Madame Soong had little or no inkling of what her husband was about; and she was so busy with her church, children, and works of charity that she did not trouble to inquire. Dr. Sun and his friends she took as a matter of course, and the conferences were to her only friendly discussions of public matters. It came as a distinct shock to her when she learned that the gentle and Christian Dr. Sun was regarded by the pillars of the old order as a dangerous criminal and that he was forced to flee to keep his head on his shoulders.

In due time what all Shanghai knew dawned upon Madame Soong—that her own husband was mixed up in the business. He was not included in the first list of those who had prices placed upon their heads, but danger always hovered over them. At last it fell, and the pious local preacher, Charles Jones Soong, had to run for his life. He took with him all members of the family who were in China at the time and escaped to Japan, where he lived for nearly two years under an assumed name in Kobe, Tokyo, and Yokohama. When the news of all this broke upon the good Madame Soong, she received it calmly; she stood by her husband and even came to share his views.

The work of propagating, organizing, and financing the Revolution in China fell more upon Soong than upon Sun. The dreamy Doctor was chased out of the country two years after he started the movement and was an exile until it began to succeed. Soong carried on in Shanghai while Sun worked abroad—organizing revolutionary societies among overseas Chinese; raising money; convening revolutionary congresses attended by thousands of Chinese students in Brussels, Berlin, Paris, and Tokyo; and in the end amalgamating all the radical societies into the one parent stem of the Kuomintang.

In 1911, during a dispute between the imperial government and business interests over the construction of a railway in Szechwan, Manchu soldiers fired upon a group of agitators and touched off the Revolution. Sun Yat-sen returned to guide the civil war and proclaimed a republic with himself as provisional president. But he soon saw that a stronger hand, especially one that controlled troops, was needed, and he made a deal with Yuan Shih-kai, commander of the imperial armies, whereby Yuan would join the Revolution and secure the abdication of the Manchus in return for the presidency. So Sun resigned in favor of Yuan, who proceeded to effect the abdication and formally set up the republic. The Soongs moved into the French Concession in Shanghai, where Sun lived with them, and Eling Soong served the Doctor as secretary. Between them the two men ran the Railway Commission, and there was constant hustling about. Great events seemed to be in store.

But things did not turn out right. The sly old Manchu retainer Yuan Shih-kai was more of the traditional war lord than an idealistic reformer. He neither understood nor loved the Revolution, and he certainly did not intend to submit to such parliamentary restraints on his own power as Sun and Soong had in mind. He plotted the overthrow of the republic, and did actually overthrow it momentarily by proclaiming himself emperor. There was a counterrevolution against Yuan, but he crushed it. The southern provinces seceded, and Sun set up a republic in the south and became president of it. So the troubled course of Chinese affairs went on.

Through all the ups and downs of the Revolution, Soong as one of its most active leaders was never entirely safe and occasionally found himself, and his family as well, in real danger. It was during an "up" period that one of his closest friends, a fellow missionary, Dr. John W. Cline, then president of Soochow University, went to see him one day at the imposing Kuomintang headquarters on Kiukiang Road, where Soong was in charge, and where Sun had an office. Reported Dr. Cline:

First I met Soon's private ricksha coolie at the street door. He was the outer bodyguard. If he hadn't recognized me, I would have got no further. After him came another bodyguard, posted at the stairway. On the second floor, a secretary stopped me outside a private office, then he went in and came out with Eling. Eling was as far as I got. Soon and Sun were having an important conference with party leaders inside. But Eling was as nice as she could be and after learning what I wanted, she said she would arrange it, and she did. A mighty smart and efficient young lady, that Eling. She's going to get somewhere in this world.

Charles Jones Soong did not live to see the success of the Revolution. When he died of stomach cancer in 1918, in mid career, aged fifty-two years, the last state of Chinese affairs was worse than the first. The fall of the Manchus had resulted in chaos. Sun Yat-sen was out of office. Yuan Shih-kai was dead, and two or three rival governments prevailed at the same time. One of them even attempted to put the twelve-year-old Manchu prince on a restored imperial throne. China had fallen apart. Yuan had placed his generals in the various provinces as governors and given them power to raise armies and money and exercise civil authority—all very well so long as Yuan lived and was maintained in power by the loyalty of these provincial *tuchuns*. But when Yuan died, the *tuchuns* felt themselves freed from subservience to any overhead government whatever, and each struck out for himself. The *tuchuns* became "war lords," each fighting the other and all fighting any general government set up by authority of the Kuomintang. That was the situation—confusion worse confounded—when Charles Jones Soong died.

3

The Soong Children Go to School

IN the house at Hongkew the Soongs lived according to the admonitions of the Lord as they understood them. It was frankly a Christian home, in which there was Bible reading, prayer, and hymn singing. Sunday school, prayer meeting, and the other services at the church were patronized faithfully. The Methodist virtues of the day were practiced, probably a little on the puritan side, but nevertheless with all good intentions and notably beneficent results. There were no dancing, no drinking, no card playing, no games on Sunday. On a ship bound for America young Eling Soong was once asked to dance, but she replied, "I am a Christian, and Christians do not dance."

Charlie Soong was a preacher with an evangelical experience, and he approved the moral discipline at home, but it was Madame Soong who inspired and directed it. She was a remarkable woman, a Spartan type, who reminds us of Susanna Wesley. Her standard for the children was to make them cultured, self-reliant, useful, and good; and she succeeded. She lived up to her distinguished ancestry in her interest in philosophy and literature, and she so abounded in good works that she became widely known as the lady who gave so much to the poor. A former teacher in Shanghai describes her as a woman who loved the people her husband served as pastor:

She was a preacher's wife who learned to love the itinerancy, who cherished the friendships of the rural women. They came

40

to her with their sick babies, and she gave them Christian medicine. She taught them about bathing and the use of soap and powder; she showed them how to boil the buffalo milk to make it clean and wholesome for their babies. She loved them, and they responded. . . . . [Even in later years] every friend of Mrs. Soong knew that in her heart she was always "preacher's wife." She came into large influence in Shanghai, and her ministry as "Mother of the Nation" was unparalleled, but the mothers still came with their babies, and she still loved to give them a cup of tea, to sit across the table from them in the room of the house which she kept furnished so simply that no one could be afraid it would be spoiled by sticky little fingers or cookie crumbs, and tell them the simple story of Jesus and the fisher folk of Galilee.[1]

Madame Soong prayed about everything, often beginning before dawn and spending hours in her prayer room on the third floor. Mayling has written that she had a feeling that, no matter what she did or did not do, her mother would "pray me through"—"And I must say that whenever mother prayed and trusted God for her decision, the undertaking invariably turned out well." One day Mayling asked her mother why she did not pray for the annihilation of the Japanese. "When you pray, or expect me to pray," was the grave reply, "don't insult God's intelligence by asking Him to do something which would be unworthy even of you, a mortal." This woman exerted a powerful and determinative influence on the children, and Mayling confesses that she groped confusedly in the dark when her mother was taken away by death. Her influence upon her children's mates was strong too. It was long her custom to bring them all home on Sunday evenings, and on those occasions Dr. Sun Yat-sen did not talk politics.

Six children were born to the Soongs: Eling, Chingling,

---

[1] Elizabeth Claiborne, "Mrs. K. T. Soong—Her Day," *The Missionary Voice*, December, 1931, p. 586.

Tse-vung (Tse-ven), Mayling, Tse-liang, Tse-an. All the world knows the first four; the two others, if not equally notable, are at least well known in China and for their years have served the country well. By marriage the girls brought into the family circle three famous men: Dr. Sun Yat-sen himself, Dr. H. H. Kung, descendent of Confucius and finance minister, and Generalissimo Chiang Kai-shek. The oldest son, known everywhere as T. V., has been both finance and foreign minister and is a great international financial statesman.

The education of the girls—Eling, Chingling, and Mayling— began early. They were taught the Chinese characters, the rudiments of the traditional culture, something about cooking, and embroidering pictures on silk. Not too much of most of this, for it did not please the girls overmuch, and it did not please their father. The Americanized father rather encouraged the tomboy spirit in his daughters; for he protected them when they made jokes about their old sewing teacher, bought Eling the first bicycle ever owned by a girl in China, and taught them to sing with him the songs he learned in Tennessee and North Carolina. So it was decided that the girls must go to McTyeire School as early as possible.

McTyeire, named for the bishop who sent Soong back to China, was then and is now the most important school of its kind in Shanghai. It was established in 1892, and was strictly in the Young J. Allen tradition in that it was intended mainly for the daughters of upper-class Chinese families. Critics were sure such families would not allow their girls to be smeared with the foreign learning, but it did not turn out so. The school was a success, and outgrew its quarters in ten years. As it was a Methodist school, of course the Soong girls must go there.

Eling was sent when she was five years old. McTyeire did

not admit babies of that age, but Charlie Soong was an important man, and the principal, Helen Richardson, was an understanding woman. Moreover, Eling herself had a way with her. When Miss Richardson asked if the baby really wanted to enter the school, Eling spoke up in perfect English and declared that she wanted it very much. So they took her on trial. She was the only baby, and there were no classes she could enter, but Miss Richardson looked after her and gave her private lessons for two years. The chairs and desks were too high, and her legs went to sleep; she could not reach the food in the center of the table, and the other girls got most of it, leaving her often hungry; she frequently was scared and lonesome in the dormitory where she slept. But Eling stuck it out and profited, and in ten years she was ready for college.

Chingling was three years younger than her sister, and in childhood was evidently not so self-reliant and assertive, since she did not enter McTyeire until she was seven years old. But the baby among the girls, Mayling, followed Eling's example and showed up at the age of five. If her own descriptions of herself are to be trusted, she did not at the time give promise of growing into the graceful beauty she actually became. She was so fat they called her "Little Lantern," and she waddled about in winter wearing cotton-padded clothes that added to her pudginess, but protected her when she fell down. She had two pigtails tied with red ribbons, and her shoes were made like cats' heads, with ears, eyes, and whiskers. But she did not endure these costumes long, for her brother T. V. began passing his clothes down to her, and she wore boys' clothes most of the time.

Mayling was taken on trial at McTyeire as Eling had been, but she did not get on so well. Her behavior was good, and there was no complaint about her studies. She was a devoted little thing and took her mother's religious precepts with considerable seriousness, for it is reported that she objected to the raising of questions in the religious discussions: "Why do you ask Pastor Li questions? Don't you believe?" But she could not stand the nights. Though she had something of a reputation for bravery, in reality she suffered from nervousness and fright and was unable to sleep in the big dormitory. When this was discovered, she was taken back to her home and placed under a private tutor.

The third Soong child was Tse-vung, now the famous T. V. He came between Chingling and Mayling. His father had fond dreams for his eldest son and gave him the name of Paul at his baptism, in the hope that he would take up the direct missionary work which the father had laid down. Missionary friends always knew the lad best as Paul. The Methodists had no school for boys in Shanghai corresponding to McTyeire for girls, but Paul must attend a Christian school, so after early preparation at home he was sent to Episcopalian St. John's University, which had special classes for quite young students.

All the children were at home during the summers, and their education continued under tutors. They went to the home of an Englishwoman in the mornings to study English and Latin; and in the afternoon an old scholar, who had tutored their father when he returned from America, came to the Soong house to give instruction in the Chinese classics. And so the Soong children grew in wisdom and stature and were duly nurtured in the fear of the Lord.

One of Charlie Soongs dearest dreams was that his children should go to America to complete their education—all of them, even the girls, a thing then unheard of. In 1903 he considered that Eling was ready for the venture, and approached his old friend and Vanderbilt classmate W. B. Burke about the matter. Burke thought the girl was too young, but he agreed to help. As girls were not expected to attend Trinity or Vanderbilt, Burke, who was from southern Georgia, recommended Wesleyan College at Macon, a Methodist college which boasted that it was the oldest chartered woman's college in the world and the first to confer a degree upon a woman. He volunteered to approach President DuPont Guerry, a personal friend, and found him willing not only to receive Eling as a student but even to take her into his own home until she became accustomed to the surroundings. Burke further promised to take Eling to America when he went home on his furlough in 1904.

Preparations for Eling's great adventure began in earnest. Mrs. J. W. Cline, a missionary neighbor, undertook the preparation of foreign clothes for her. One difficulty was her passport. The American exclusion laws shut out Oriental immigrants; and though they did not apply to students, there was great nervousness on the point among the Chinese themselves. Soong bethought him of the expedient of securing a Portuguese passport. James Burke intimates that the Portuguese sold such documents to anyone and that Soong himself had previously bought one to escape execution by the imperial authorities.[2] The woman who actually brought Eling to America says that Soong claimed he was born in Macao, a Portuguese possession, and that his children were therefore entitled to Portuguese citizenship. At any rate he got the passport.

The Burke family and their charge left Shanghai on May 28, 1904, on the Pacific Mail steamer "Korea"; the steamer also carried more than five hundred boxes of opium and picked up two million dollars worth of gold—and Jack London—in

[2] *My Father in China*, pp. 197, 229.

Japan. Unfortunately, Mrs. Burke fell desperately ill and had to be removed to a hospital at Yokohama, where she died. A dilemma was thus created as to what should be done about Eling.

What happened has been variously reported. James Burke says his father turned her over to another missionary couple on board, who hurt her feelings by an offensive remark about "dirty Chinamen and those awful Japs" and deserted her when her entry was delayed at San Francisco; that she fell in with a "Miss Lanman" from Korea who took her in charge and stayed with her through all her vicissitudes in connection with the customs regulations.[3] Emily Hahn says that Burke delivered her to "another missionary, a Korean woman of the Burkes' acquaintance," who was going to America to visit her sick father, and who treated her kindly and remained with her loyally during her San Francisco detention, Eling's troubles being caused by the fact that her passport indicated she was traveling with an American family whereas she was actually in the company of another Oriental.[4]

But a first-hand account is now given by the guardian angel herself—Mrs. S. A. Stewart, a missionary in Japan until the approach of war forced her withdrawal in 1941. Mrs. Stewart —then Miss Anna Lanius—says she was going home from Japan on the "Korea" for her first furlough when Burke asked her assistance because she was the only other Southern Methodist on the ship. She was assured that Eling's papers were all correct and that the girl had plenty of money, but when they returned from going ashore at Honolulu the purser or a steward informed her that the girl's papers were defective and trouble might be expected at San Francisco.

---

[3] *Ibid.,* pp. 235-38.
[4] *The Soong Sisters,* p. 48.

Trouble came. Eling was refused admission to the United States when she presented her Portuguese passport. One of the inspectors, a Dr. Gardner, who had been a missionary in Canton, said the detention house in San Francisco "was not fit for a self-respecting animal" and that the girl could remain on the ship until another vessel could take her back to China. Miss Lanius stayed with her. The ship was dismantled; carpets were taken up; bedding was turned out to be cleaned. The two lonely prisoners were fed beefsteak, potatoes, and cold bread three times a day.

Dr. C. F. Reid, the missionary who had officiated at Charlie Soong's wedding in China, was in San Francisco at the time as superintendent of work among Orientals along the coast. He went to the ship to see the daughter of his old friend but was called away by a week-end engagement, unaware of the difficulties about her passport. On the third day Miss Lanius, who had reached a state of near-collapse, was given permission to go ashore and telephone to Dr. Reid, whom she reached by the help of the workers in a Presbyterian home for Chinese women. On the following day Reid came to the ship with a trained nurse, who took charge of Eling and allowed Miss Lanius to proceed to her home in Missouri. For two weeks more, a total of nineteen days, Eling remained in custody and was transferred from one ship to another until Dr. Reid was able to establish connections in Washington and arrange for her entrance into the country.

Mrs. Stewart remembers Eling, who was called by the American name of Alice, as "a well-behaved young girl with a correct knowledge of English and a good vocabulary." As the ship sailed into the San Francisco harbor she exclaimed, "Aren't the people afraid to live on hills like that?" When the cargo was being unloaded she was surprised to see "white men doing coolies' work."

Once she said there seemed to be no place for her anywhere—in China she was a Christian and therefore different from other people, and in America she was not wanted. But there would be a change in China someday—people were always coming to talk to her father about it. I did not attach much importance to that remark then, but six years later the "change" began.[5]

Eling did not forget the indignities imposed upon her by the customs officers. A year later she was taken to Washington to see her uncle, Wan Bing-chung, who was in America at the head of a Chinese educational commission, and had the honor of being presented to Theodore Roosevelt at the White House. The young girl told the President of her experience in no uncertain terms, and pointed out that in China no visitor would ever be subjected to such treatment.

After landing, Eling remained in San Francisco three days awaiting the arrival of Burke, who proceeded on another ship after the burial of his wife in Yokohama. They went to Macon together, arriving on the night of August 2. The Macon newspaper announced the arrival of "the Chinese girl who was detained aboard ship at San Francisco while on her way to Wesleyan College" and reported, "The girl is said to be quite a bright one." President Guerry was quoted as follows: "Of course she will not force herself or be forced upon any of the other young ladies as an associate. They will be free and can conduct themselves as they see fit. I have no misgivings as to her kind and respectful treatment."

Any such misgivings would have been entirely unjustified, for Eling won the student body and townspeople by her gracious manner and charming personality, and for five years was one of the most popular girls in the college. She enrolled in the subfreshman class and lived in the home of the president during the whole of the first year, taking up her ac-

---

[5] From personal letters of Mrs. Stewart to the author

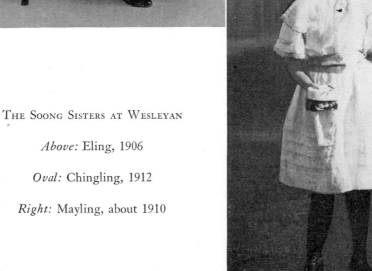

THE SOONG SISTERS AT WESLEYAN

Above: Eling, 1906

Oval: Chingling, 1912

Right: Mayling, about 1910

1908-1909

The act of subscribing by name below implies a solemn promise on my part that I will faithfully keep all the rules and regulations of the WESLEYAN FEMALE COLLEGE, so long as I remain a pupil in-the Institution.

No.	NAME	AGE	DATE OF ENTRY	PARENTS OR GUARDIAN	POST OFFICE	COUNTY	State	CLASS	COURSE
1	Martha Drake	16	Sept. 9th	Mrs. J. & Javier	Macon, Ga	Bibb.	Ga	Special	Piano & Voice
2	Eoling Soong	18	Sept. 5th	Mr. C. J. Soong	Shanghai	China	China	Senior	Piano(?)
3	May Ling Soong	10	Sept. 5th	Mr. C. J. Soong	Shanghai	China	China		
4	Ching Ling Soong	15	Sept. 6th	Mr. C. J. Soong	Shanghai	China	China		
5	Jesse C. Sutton	17	"	Mr. C. L. Earnest	Bartow, Fla	Polk Co.	Fla		

SIGNATURES OF THE SOONGS IN THE WESLEYAN MATRICULATION BOOK

customed religious activities at the near-by Mulberry Street Church. Her environment at home had accustomed her to many phases of American life, and she dropped with only minor difficulties into the manners of the country, wearing American clothes and dressing her hair according to the American pattern. During the summers she traveled extensively and attended summer schools at various places. At a party in New York she met a Yale postgraduate student named Kung Hsiang-hsi, but he made so little impression that he dropped completely out of her mind.

In 1908 came Chingling's turn to go to Wesleyan. She was a studious sort of girl with a high idealism and a serious interest in moral and philosophic matters even at the early age of fifteen. When the usual preparations for her departure were under way the baby, Mayling, declared she wanted to go along. She was only ten, and of course much too young to enter college, or even to leave home; but it seems that on a certain medicine-taking occasion her parents had made elaborate promises, and Mayling now held them to their word. So she went. Both girls were under the care of aunt and uncle Wan, who were bringing a party of Chinese students to America on the steamer "Manchuria," and they passed the immigration barrier at San Francisco without special incident.

Eling was a senior that year and able to ease her sisters' adjustment to the new environment. Like Eling the two younger girls adopted not only American clothes and manners but also American names—Chingling became Rosamond and Mayling simply May. They already spoke English fluently; they had learned it in their home and perfected it at McTyeire. Since Charlie Soong had been trained in North Carolina and Tennessee and McTyeire was a Southern Methodist institution, it took little time in Georgia to mold their speech into the soft and liquid accent of the South—so charming when natural, so terrible when imitated. They imbibed also the Southern courtesy and traditions; it is said that when Mayling was later asked by a teacher at a northern summer school to describe Sherman's raid through Georgia she replied with dignity, "I am a Southerner, and that subject is very painful to me."

At the end of their year together, Eling graduated—with high honors though only nineteen. The class prophecy declared she would be the wife of the greatest reformer China had ever had and the real power behind the throne. The three went to Demorest, Georgia, for a summer vacation; and when the time came for Eling to return to China and Chingling to Wesleyan, Mayling liked the town so well she wanted to stay. Accordingly, she was left for the following school year in the care of Mrs. Moss, mother of one of Eling's classmates and matron of the boys' dormitory at Piedmont College, where Mayling was forthwith entered as a pupil in the eighth grade of the preparatory department.

Many of the Piedmont College students came from the hill country, where educational opportunities were limited, and some of eleven-year-old Mayling's classmates were actually adults. In a later reminiscence of her stay in Demorest she has written how this impressed her:

I began to get an insight into the lives of those who had to struggle for a living and for even the means to acquire an elementary education. I suppose my contact with these people as a girl influenced my interest in the lot of those who were not born with a silver spoon in their mouths, a contact which I may never have experienced otherwise. It made me see their sterling worth because, after all, they and their kind constitute the backbone of any nation.

At Piedmont Mayling studied arithmetic and made poor

grades, she recalls, in percentages and discounts. She did better in English grammar and rhetoric, and in physiology came off with a 98 and was exempted from the final examination. The village people found her something of a curiosity, but she seems to have experienced little self-consciousness. She ate gumdrops at Hunt's general store, hunted hazelnuts and blackberries in the woods, thumbed rides from the farmers on their wagons, read on a wooden bench between two trees in front of the boys' dormitory, studied piano under Rosina Moss, ate hot cakes with blackberry jam, and had the earache.

When Mayling returned to Macon with Chingling the following year, she found that during her absence Wesleyan had acquired a new president—Dr. William N. Ainsworth, later a bishop and superintendent of the China Mission. Dr. and Mrs. Ainsworth had a daughter, Eloise, two years younger than Mayling, who became her constant companion. Another playmate was Marjorie Gugel, now Mrs. Homer Key. They formed a sorority in imitation of the older girls and initiated Dr. Ainsworth and various members of the faculty, and for a time they edited and published a daily newspaper with a circulation of five copies, all different. Many in Macon today remember Mayling as a beautiful, vivacious, lovable, and popular child, full of life and what our fathers called, not too approvingly, "animal spirits."

Since Mayling was not ready for even the subfreshman classes at Wesleyan, she was tutored during the next two years by a member of the faculty, Miss Margie Burks, whose mother, Mrs. M. M. Burks, professor of English, became a sort of guardian angel or foster mother to the child. During the summers she traveled in other parts of the country, sometimes with Chingling and sometimes with others. At length, in the fall of 1912, she was admitted to Wesleyan as a bona fide student. She was elected sergeant-at-arms of her class and carried the banner and led the cheering on occasions when such activities were indicated. In the college annual for 1913 her picture appears with the information that she was a member of the tennis club and the Billy Crows; all that is remembered of the latter organization is that its members met at the "crow's nest," ate licorice, and adopted the black tulip as the club flower.

The same year T. V. Soong broke the family educational tradition by enrolling in Harvard University. T. V. and Mayling had always been pals; and when Chingling graduated in the spring of 1913 and prepared to return to China, it was deemed best that the young sister should go north and be near him. So Mayling went to Wellesley and entered the freshman class. If we are to believe the reports put out by the college after she had become its most notable alumna—and there is ample independent evidence to support them—she was an excellent student, very popular, and made a rather unusual record. She majored in English literature with a minor in philosophy, and studied languages, elocution, science, and the Bible. She was a member of Tau Zeta Epsilon, a local sorority; and at her graduation she was designated as a "Durant Scholar," the highest academic distinction at Wellesley. She lived at Wood Cottage and kept a rather terrifying Oriental sword hanging on the wall.

Mayling Soong graduated from Wellesley in 1917. She had been away from home during nine formative years of her life. She had been all over America and had mixed with many kinds of people. She had all but forgotten the Shanghai dialect, and when she returned to China she had to learn to read and write. "The only thing Oriental about me is my face," she said; but it was not strictly true, for many persons thought she did not even look very much like a Chinese.

4

The Kungs, the Suns, and the Soongs

ELING SOONG returned to Shanghai in 1910, a cultured and beautiful young woman of twenty, full of the democratic ideals she had imbibed in America. She found her father deep in the intrigues of the Revolution, and the liberal ideas which had meant little to her six years before were now full of meaning and promise for China. There was prejudice against such as she in those days; the old-order conservatives disliked foreign-educated women, foreign clothes, foreign speech, and the aggressiveness that went with such things. But Eling Soong, though more sensitive and shy than her two younger sisters, carried bravely on, brushed up on her Shanghai dialect, and gave little cause for ill-natured gossip on the part of the conservatives. She became secretary to Dr. Sun Yat-sen and was soon as deep in the Revolution as anybody else.

She had met Kung Hsiang-hsi—better known as H. H. Kung—in America when he was a student there. He had already experienced some adventures. He was born in 1881 in Taiku, Shansi province, of an old and distinguished family of bankers. The Kungs traced a direct line back to the great Confucius, Hsiang-hsi being the seventy-fifth lineal descendant, and this fact gave the family a place of honor among all Chinese. In boyhood he came in touch with an American medical missionary and was converted to Christianity. He was sent to school in Peking and was there when the Boxer trouble broke out. He had never heard of Dr. Sun, but he became a revolutionist at heart and hated the Manchu empress. There is a story to the effect that he joined up with other young men and financed a plan to bribe a palace eunuch and thus secure access to the empress and murder her. The Boxer rebellion came just at that moment, and the scheme fell through.

The story goes on to say that in the ensuing excitement Kung hastened to the aid of some missionaries with whom he was friendly and whose lives were endangered. They were killed, but they gave the young man some letters for transmission to America. He carried the dangerous missives on his person and in spite of hazards and difficulties managed to reach his home. There he called the family together, confessed that he was a Christian, told about the letters, and declared he must leave to avoid being a menace to the home folks. They were outraged but would not let him go, smuggling him by night from one place to another while the old grandmother took care of the letters. All survived the rebellion and Hsiang-hsi in due course delivered the letters to America. Such is the story.

Anyway, Kung did go to America, where he graduated from Oberlin in 1906 and took an M.A. degree at Yale the following year. He returned to China and tried to organize a modern school in Taiku, but the Revolution occurred and he became commander of the revolutionary troops in Shansi. Young men with foreign training were in demand then, and Kung was offered diplomatic jobs and the governorship of the province, but he stuck to his idea of building a school. But the defection of Yuan Shih-kai and the counterrevolution against him indicated that Kung might well go to Japan, where both Sun and Soong had gone. He became secretary of the Chinese Y. M. C. A. in Tokyo.

In Japan he first met Sun Yat-sen, whose principles he by

this time knew and accepted. He met Soong also, and was invited home to dinner when he recalled meeting Eling in New York. Eling paid more attention to the young man this time, and a romance was soon under way. Kung had been married before, in a childhood family-arranged affair, but his wife had died. So Eling became his wife in a Christian ceremony performed in a church at Yokohama.

The Kungs went to Taiku and lived in the great Kung house there, and Madame Kung overcame her shyness to the extent of becoming a teacher in the school which finally got under way. Hsiang-hsi undertook business ventures and prospered, secured a monopoly on American oil in Shansi, acquired valuable properties in his province and in Shanghai, and eventually became one of the richest men in all China. They did not remain in Shansi, but moved to Peking, Shanghai, and elsewhere as duty called them.

The Kungs have four children: Rosamond, born in Taiku; and David, Jeannette, and Louis, born in Shanghai. The birth of Rosamond in 1916 was so nearly fatal to both mother and child that it drove Madame Kung more deeply into her mother's religious faith. She had been a serious girl and always interested in the church and the work of the missionaries. While at Wesleyan she had written a paper in which she warned the church of the danger of exposing to the subtleties of Chinese philosophy any missionaries who were not deeply grounded in Christian experience and faith. But she had never been as pious as Madame Soong desired. Now the influence of her training returned, and she had a feeling that the hand of God had intervened to save her life and that of her child, for which she gave Him fervent and grateful praise. She believes that she "became a genuine Christian at that time." She wanted to give the Soong home to the church, but her sisters and brothers did not approve, and it was kept intact and cared for by the old servants even after all the Soongs had left it. When the war came, she became as noted for good works as her mother had been.

More and more Dr. Kung entered into public life and accepted the responsibilities which his wealth and abilities brought. He became much, and naturally, interested in Oberlin-in-China and served on the directing boards of numerous banks, educational institutions, and philanthropic organizations. He received honorary degrees from colleges in China and other lands. He has held more important posts than any other Chinese in contemporary history—president of the Executive Yuan, finance minister, member of the Central Political Council of the Kuomintang, the National Defense Commission, the National Economic Council, the Overseas Affairs Commission, and a score of others.

As these honors and duties came to her husband, Madame Kung could not pursue the life of simple domesticity which she preferred. She accompanied Dr. Kung to America in 1932 when he went as special industrial commissioner, and after enduring the necessary round of official functions, she slipped away and went to Macon. From all over Georgia her old Wesleyan friends came back to meet her. She was gloriously happy in their companionship, but she cried until aromatic spirits of ammonia had to be brought when admiring newspapers published comments she considered extravagant. Judge Guerry, who had been so kind to her, and whom she loved as a father, had passed away; Madame Kung went with Mrs. Guerry to the cemetery, knelt at his grave, and left an armful of roses. Later she established a scholarship at Wesleyan in his memory. Her son David was with her on the trip, and they left Dr. Kung behind and returned leisurely to China by way of Europe.

It was the war which forced Madame Kung completely out

of her shyness and gave her a place among the great women of China. When during the Japanese aggression of 1932 wounded soldiers had begun pouring into Shanghai, where the Kungs were then living, she had induced three friends to join her in giving $80,000 to fit out a small hospital and then had organized a drive to finance a larger one. With the start of the full-scale hostilities in 1937 her sympathy entirely overcame her self-consciousness. She organized the leading women and girls to serve the soldiers and did more than any other person to change the traditional Chinese attitude of indifference or contempt toward soldiers into one of sympathy and appreciation. As the war drew nearer to Shanghai, her activities increased. She bought ambulances and trucks with her own money, took over a prominent cabaret and converted it into a hospital, and purchased clothing for the soldiers. When the government at last took refuge in Chungking, she allowed herself to be persuaded to fly there in company with her two sisters. As they had not seen much of each other, and there had been a degree of estrangement, which rumor had greatly magnified, the presence of the three famous women together in the ruins of war had an electrical effect throughout the nation and greatly strengthened Chinese morale. She even broadcast several messages to America and the world, as did her sisters. She has supported the co-operatives, the New Life Movement, the orphans, the missionary projects, and all the patriotic and Christian causes which the war has brought forth.

When Chingling graduated and returned to China in 1913, she brought a box of fruit for Dr. Sun Yat-sen. She had been something of a revolutionist at Wesleyan. On one occasion she received from her father a flag of the new republic; she promptly tore the old imperial dragon flag from her wall and stamped on it, substituted the new one, and cried, "Down with the dragon; up with the flag of the Republic!" In her junior year she contributed to the college magazine an article on the Revolution entitled, "The Greatest Event of the Twentieth Century."

She found her family living in a house on Avenue Joffre in the French Concession at Shanghai, Dr. Sun and her father running the Railway Commission and shuttling back and forth between Shanghai and Nanking, Sun living in the Soong house, and Eling serving as the great man's secretary. She wrote to her friends in Macon that she wore American clothes and that Shanghai was in many ways more modern than Atlanta, and she inquired whether the "old maids" in her class were "waiting or baiting." She had known Sun since childhood as a friend of the family, and what she had heard and read of him in the meantime had caused her to regard him as a conquering hero. When, during the exile in Japan, Eling married Dr. Kung, Sun asked Chingling to be his secretary, and shortly thereafter she dumfounded her family by announcing her engagement to the Leader.

The Soongs and their friends were so upset because everything except the desires of the contracting parties themselves was against the match. They now encountered the perplexing situation which has arisen so often when Christian conceptions encounter the traditional views and practices of the non-Christian world. Sun was already married and had three children. It had been a childhood marriage, and with all his running about in the world Sun had paid little or no attention to his wife in recent years; but both he and his wife were Christians, and Sun could not plead that the marriage was only a hangover from a repudiated heathenism.

Dr. Sun had not even divorced his wife. Even had he done so the situation would not have been bettered; since she had given no cause for complaint, the putting away of a faithful wife to marry a girl half his age would have contravened the Christian morality so cherished by Madame Soong. It was a bitter dose, but the Soongs had to swallow it with what grace they could. Sun and Chingling were determined, and while the arguments went on she left home and joined him. She wrote a Wesleyan friend that they were married in "the simplest possible" manner, "for we both hate surplus ceremonies."

There were all kinds of reactions to the marriage. Sun Fo, the Doctor's son, who was in America studying journalism, was so incredulous when he heard the news that he denied it in a newspaper interview. But he offered his services to his father's government when he returned to China and was made secretary of the National Assembly. The Soongs and the missionaries deplored it, and the old guard were frankly scandalized. But the young liberals endorsed it and were ecstatic over their Leader's marriage to the beautiful and edu cated daughter of his best friend in defiance of the outmoded prejudices of the oldsters.

The Suns returned to China from the exile in Japan and lived in their house on Rue Molière in Shanghai. In 1920 they went to Canton where Sun was president of a "republic" with only one province. In the rest of China the Revolution had not gone well, and everything was in confusion as factional leaders struggled with each other and presidents and "governments" rose and fell. Li Yuan-hung became president when Yuan Shih-kai died and made some attempt to set up a representative government; but he had a dispute with the prime minister, General Tuan Chi-jui, and Chang Hsun entered Peking and tried to place the Manchu boy-prince, Hsun Tung, on the throne. This was suppressed, and then Li resigned the presidency to General Feng Kuo-chang, who was soon ousted, and the reactionary Hsu Shih-chang came on. In 1919 the premier, Tuan Chi-jui, was driven out by Wu Pei-fu and Chang Tso-lin; then Wu drove out Chang, only to be driven out himself by the "Christian General," Feng Yu-hsiang, who called General Tuan back.

The southern provinces of China took little part in all this. They seceded from the Peking regime and proclaimed a republic of their own. Here Sun was recognized, the Kuomintang developed, an army was trained; and from here deliverance eventually came.

Though his prestige was lost in the North, Sun was a distinguished figure in the South, and his young and glamorous wife shared his glory. She was nearly as shy as her older sister and disliked too much prominence, but it was thrust upon her none the less. Many legends grew up: she wrote to friends in America that reports had been circulated in Macon that she was a spy of the revolutionists even before her marriage.

She was not allowed to have peace even in Canton. Sun got together some members of the old Peking parliament and had himself elected "President of China." Then, thinking his republic should have at least one more province, he sent his general, Chen Chiung-ming, out to take Kwangsi, which Chen did. Then Sun wanted to start northward, but Chen refused to march, and Sun dismissed him.

Factions were created in the South by such tactics, and Chen started a revolt which drove out Sun and nearly cost the life of Madame Sun. Chen's troops invaded and looted Canton. Sun rushed back from the northern expedition he was sponsoring, but the situation was out of hand, and he escaped to a warship. The presidential residence was fired on, and Madame Sun escaped by the breadth of a hair. Several days she was in danger of death, with bullets flying about her, a roof shot off over her head, her guards killed at her side. At last she managed to reach a wayside cottage from which she finally emerged to safety disguised as a countrywoman carrying a basket of vegetables. She reached Shanghai, and her husband joined her after two years.

About this time Dr. Sun lined up with Russia. He had been unable to obtain help for the Revolution from any other nation, though he tried many, but Russia courted him. Revolution was to the liking of the Bolshevik regime of the period. The Russian ambassador came down from Peking and agreed with Sun on a policy of co-operation: Communism was not to be established in China, but the Chinese would have the sympathy and support of Russia, and the Soviets would give up their special rights in China—which the United States and Great Britain did not do until 1942, when such rights had been lost anyway. The relinquishment of extraterritoriality seemed proof of Russia's good intentions and won the approval of many Chinese for Sun's policy. On the last day of 1923 the Doctor announced: "We no longer look to the Western Powers. Our faces are turned toward Russia."

Michael Borodin was sent by the Bolsheviks to be chief adviser to Sun and the revolutionary movement. Russian officers trained Sun's soldiers. Chinese Communists were admitted as members of the Kuomintang. Russian agents surrounded Sun. When he died they disputed with his Christian wife over a Christian burial ceremony; the Russian flag was the first to be lowered to half mast; and the Russians alone sent a minister to his funeral. His body was held three weeks waiting for a casket from Russia, which was too shabby to use when it at last arrived.

Neither Dr. Sun nor Madame Sun ever accepted Communism. Its principles were not espoused in *San Min Chu I*, the bible of the Kuomintang which was compiled by Sun during his last days. On one occasion he drew a circle labeled "Kuomintang," inside of which he placed Communism, Capitalism, and all the other isms which he felt had ideas good for China—a gesture which sufficiently explained his attitude. He would take from every source anything that would contribute to the success of the Revolution and the ultimate betterment of China.

Four months before his death, things looked brighter for Sun. General Feng invited the Doctor to come to Peking for a conference with those in power there, presumably with ideas of conciliation and unification in mind. He had previously been invited to come by Wu Pei-fu, but had refused because he did not trust Wu. Now he consented, and he and Madame Sun started in November. He was a sick man, and although the trip was leisurely he was at the point of death when he arrived, from cancer of the liver. He died in the home of Dr. Wellington Koo in Peking on March 12, 1925, at the age of fifty-eight. Chingling was with him, as were his daughter and Sun Fo.

The funeral involved some three weeks of public mourning with a series of ceremonies by various groups. Certain party officials declared there should be no religious rites, on the ground that the Leader belonged to China as a whole and not to any one creed, and there were even threats of violent reactions to such a service; but the family nevertheless insisted on a Christian funeral. Madame Sun herself selected the hymns, "Jesus, Lover of My Soul," "Crossing the Bar," and "Wonderful Words of Life," and asked that they be sung by a vested choir, since Dr. Sun had sung in a choir as a boy. The service was conducted in the chapel of the Peking Union Medical College by a teacher, Dr. Timothy Tingfang Lew. As minister and choir led the procession across the campus and the street, radicals with stones in their hands mingled with the throngs, but no untoward incident occurred. Nor were later reactions anything but favorable, or at least neutral. It is told that some years later in one of the western provinces a meeting to initiate a violent anti-Christian campaign was broken up when an account and a picture of Dr. Sun's funeral were shown.

Sun Yat-sen became almost a god after his death. Those who gave him no administrative support while he lived accepted and quoted his words as gospel after he died. His mantle fell on his wife—the mantle of his ideals, for he left nothing else behind him. His writings, like those of any gospel, are capable of many interpretations, and she became a sort of authoritative commentary on the revolutionary program.

Her loyalty to the letter of her great husband's loyalties led her to a long estrangement—official, not personal—from other members of her family. When Generalissimo Chiang Kai-shek, always a loyal and trusted friend of Dr. Sun and the Revolution, at last undertook to subdue the provincial war lords and unify China under Kuomintang rule, the Communists gave him trouble. His army was full of them. As he marched northward from Canton, Borodin went along; and in his rear followed a host of organizers, propagandists, and agitators. When Nanking was taken, the army got out of hand and committed many outrages, looting missionary residences and institutions, consulates, and the whole city, and shooting the American president of Nanking University. The Generalissimo attributed this to the Communists and kicked them all out, including Michael Borodin. The Kuomintang was thus disrupted. Chiang set up a Nationalist government at Nanking, and the Communist sympathizers formed one of their own at Hankow.

This gave deep offense to Madame Sun. The Kungs and T. V. Soong sided with Chiang, but the Leader's widow was bitter against his treatment of the Russians, with whom she had been working since her husband's death. She returned to her house in Shanghai for a time and then went to Moscow, giving out a public statement in which she declared that "some members of the party executive" had done "violence to Dr. Sun's ideas and ideals," and that therefore "I must disassociate myself from active participation in carrying out the new policies of the party." In her exile she brooded on what had happened and gave out a statement still more bitter.

There have been betrayals and a complete distorting of the Nationalist movement. . . . . The greatest blot upon China is that this shameful counterrevolution is being led by men who have been intimately associated in the public mind with the Nationalist movement. . . . . These men, having alienated the people, are trying again to drag China along the familiar road of petty feudalistic wars for personal gain and power.

In Russia she was lonely, ill, and sometimes in poverty; but she refused all aid from her family, who constantly begged her to return to China. She went to Switzerland for her health, then to Berlin, always grieving for her idol and her country.

She returned in the spring of 1929 to attend the state burial of Dr. Sun Yat-sen. His body had been kept in a temple at Peking and was now to be removed to the great mausoleum erected for it on Purple Mountain at Nanking. But she made it plain that she was going only to perform a widow's sad duty, and that she adhered to her statement disassociating herself from the Nationalist regime under Chiang Kai-shek. Asked why she was so bitter towards a government in which her own family was so influential, she is said to have remarked that the Soongs existed for China and not China for the

Left: MADAME H. H. KUNG

Keystone View Co.

Right: H. H. KUNG

Upper left: SUN YAT-SEN

Upper right: MADAME SUN YAT-SEN

Lower left: T. V. SOONG

Soongs. But she remained personally on good terms with Mayling and uttered no word against the Kungs. She kept apart from them during the elaborate ceremonials that attended the enshrinement of her husband's body and then went to her house in Shanghai. Then she sent to Berlin a telegram which was a blast indeed:

While the oppressed nationalities today form a solid front against imperialist war and militarism, the reactionary Nanking Government is combining forces with the Imperialists in brutal repressions against the Chinese masses. Never has the treacherous character of the counterrevolutionary Kuomintang leaders been so shamelessly exposed to the world as today. Having betrayed the Nationalist revolution, they have inevitably degenerated into imperialist tools and attempted to provoke war with Russia.

This message was suppressed in China. Only one paper mentioned it, and a man who tried to distribute it in leaflet form was arrested.

In 1932 George E. Sokolsky wrote in *The New York Times Magazine:*

For Mme. Sun the world stopped moving when Dr. Sun Yat-sen died. To her, his ideals, his plans, his principles have become a faith. She alone now holds ever before the Chinese people his vision, as he saw it, as they saw it together. Practical considerations of policy and the needs of the State do not to her justify deviations from the wishes of the Master. . . . . Alone she stands and beckons the nation back to Dr. Sun Yat-sen. The response is scant as yet; but her sincerity and honesty shine like mighty suns of hope over bleak China of today.

Madame Sun went to Europe, returned to Shanghai, and, when the Japanese came, went to Hongkong, where the

Kungs were living. It was the Japanese invasion and the threat to China's independent existence which eventually caused her to warm up toward Chiang Kai-shek, whose magnificent leadership could leave no doubt as to his devotion to the country. In a public statement in 1938 she referred to him as "Comrade Chiang Kai-shek," and said, "The entire nation should support and abide by the order of the Generalissimo."

A few months later reunion between the famous Soong sisters came about under stress of war, and China was thrilled. Mayling, living at Chungking under constant bombing, had been ill, and a rest was ordered. She went to Hongkong to be with Madame Kung, and Madame Sun moved into the Kung house also. At long last the sisters were again together; differences were forgotten, and the dear past was lived over in jokes, gossip, and reminiscences. They went together to a hotel and dined in public, amazing all Hongkong. Mayling insisted that her sisters should accompany her back to Chungking, and by perseverance she had her way. They flew from Hongkong to Chungking on the first day of April, 1940.

They were given a rousing welcome and were officially entertained everywhere. They went over the beleaguered capital, clambering over the debris of the bombings, going down into the deep shelters, visiting the schools, the hospitals, the orphanages, making speeches and recordings, broadcasting to America, posing for photographs. It was more than a reunion of three famous women; it was a historic occasion.

And so the widow of China's great revolutionary dreamer has again entered actively into the service of her people and is carrying on in various phases of wartime service. She has

gathered a thousand "guerrilla babies"—children in the iso-
lated mountain region of northwest China whose fathers are
in the guerrilla bands or the regular army, and whose mothers
are in war work—in day nurseries and has been instrumental
in establishing a dozen or more schools for them, including
a technical training school. In all this she is probably actuated
more by her idealism and love of country than by motives
more directly religious, but her passionate devotion to the
principles of Sun Yat-sen has something of religious zeal in
it, and she would claim that the social aims of the Revolution
are all fundamentally Christian. And she would be right.
Charlie Soong certainly would approve.

T. V. Soong finished his economics course at Harvard in
1915, having entered as a sophomore from St. John's. Want-
ing to learn all he could of his chosen specialty in America,
he got a job with an international banking house in New
York; and when his duties seemed too limited, he demanded
and obtained transfer to "more varied work." At the same
time he took graduate courses in finance at Columbia University. Deciding after a time that he had gone as far as
he could in New York, he returned to China and went to
work for a coal and iron company.

His big chance came in 1924 when Chiang Kai-shek was
at Canton with Dr. Sun preparing for his later push northward to unify China under one central government. Chiang
had no money; taxes were uncertain under the old system of
collection through numerous middlemen, which dribbled most
of the money out before it reached the treasury. Madame
Sun suggested that the General call in her young brother
and test out the financial training he had received in America.
It worked. T. V. became director of the Department of
Commerce, then general manager of the Central Bank,

then finance minister in the Nationalist government. He overhauled the entire fiscal system of China by methods as direct and frank as those employed by his father. He was hard, but fair and honest. He abolished a lot of indefensible taxes and levied taxes that the people could understand and pay. He fired an army of corrupt politicians and middlemen, and eliminated the traditional Chinese "squeeze" or graft. Citizens began to pay willingly, and what they paid reached the treasury. Revenue went up from one million to ten million dollars; the nearly worthless Canton currency rose in the markets; and the credit of the regime was established. T. V. financed the war which Chiang fought.

In 1941 an article by Ernest O. Hauser in the magazine *Life* revealed two interesting stories about T. V.'s financial and political enterprises. One relates to the break between the Generalissimo and the Communists, which has always been attributed to the outrages committed by the Red elements in Chiang's army at Nanking. As the revolutionary armies marched northward, according to this version, the Borodin group of Soviet advisers surrounding Chiang urged the Generalissimo to seize the vast stores of silver in the banks of Shanghai and defy not only the international bankers but the foreign armies which were in Shanghai for the protection of American, British, and French interests. Chiang was a military man unversed in political diplomacy; but Soong was wise enough to know that any such procedure would estrange the rest of the world, brand Chiang as a looter, clinch the grip of the Russians on China, and bring about the collapse of the whole movement for freedom. He resolved upon a coup of his own.

T. V. went into Shanghai and made a deal with the bankers, who were shivering in fear of Communism and dreading the collapse of the whole economic structure. They were not to wait until the Reds brought about the looting of their vaults. They should, on the other hand, give the money to T. V. to be used in backing Chiang Kai-shek, who on his part would kick out the Reds and set up a normal economic system. The bankers agreed, and Soong went to Chiang with three million dollars in cash as a sort of first payment. It was not necessary to take the Shanghai banks by force, for they had already been taken by diplomacy. Chiang saw the point, and Borodin and his whole Red company were shipped back to Russia. So it was really the son of Charlie Soong who saved China from going Communist.

The other story is that of the hundred million dollar loan secured by T. V. from the United States in 1940. It seems that he went about this matter with all the Soong directness. He took a taxi alone to the White House and told the President that he had "a bill of goods" to sell for a hundred million dollars; he refused to lobby and insisted that he had a business proposition and was not on a begging mission. The President called in his financial manager, Jesse Jones, and to them T. V. offered his bargain. For one hundred million dollars China would keep Japan engaged and delay the attack upon the United States until this country could prepare itself to meet the attack when it came. "The merchandise was fantastically cheap at that price," and the President, Jones, and Congress "bought" it. T. V. walked out with two fifty million dollar checks, one to curb inflation and support Chinese currency and the other to buy the materials of war. Mr. Hauser comments that this loan

hit China like 100,000,000 volts of electricity. Peace talk ceased. The inflation seemed less immediate. The Communist trouble was brought to issue. While previous grants from the U. S. ($70,000,000) had been given on a strictly pound-of-flesh basis, and had already been partly paid back in such vital raw materials as tung oil, tungsten, and tin, the Chinese knew that this new investment was downright political. The U. S. was clearly on their side.

The direct and frank tongue of T. V. Soong, in striking contrast to the roundabout indirectness of the old Chinese, has created an impression that this son of Charlie Soong is rude and irascible, but it has a persuasiveness all its own, as the big deal with America proved. When Generalissimo Chiang Kai-shek was captured, T. V. took an airplane and flew to the stronghold of the rebels and did much to secure the release of his brother-in-law. The refractory elements accused Chiang and the government of a policy of appeasement toward Japan and insisted on total war against the aggressors. T. V. convinced them that they were all wrong, that waiting was necessary to gain time for preparation.

It was in that hour [says Mr. Hauser] that China's united front . . . . was born. T. V. emerged as the father of that united front and his formidable personality has held it together. The Red Armies . . . . might have turned against the conservative officialdom of Chungking long ago if it had not been for T. V. They bowed to him because they remembered that he, the "capitalist," had stood for resistance against Japan at a time when his brother-in-law had . . . . shown many inclinations toward appeasement.

But T. V. Soong has had his own problems with the government directed by his own family. In 1933, for example, he was ousted from the office of finance minister, and brother-in-law Kung was installed in his place. Critics talked about "rival ambitions" and hinted at actual enmity; and more careful observers were mystified by the shift which replaced so shrewd a financier in the ministry, though Kung had laurels in that field and his family had been in the business for generations. But T. V. had disagreed with the financial policy of the Generalissimo, who wanted to raise more money for the army and grant large subsidies to the generals of the provinces. Probably T. V. remembered the old *tuchuns*. Anyway he insisted on reducing the national debt and resigned.

Later he resigned as head of the Chinese Air Force, a place inherited by him from his little sister, Madame Chiang Kai-shek. He found a mess of old Chinese traditional blunders. Aviators had been placed in the service because of their connections rather than in consideration of their abilities, and a group of planes had remained on the ground two years because the flyers would not man them until somebody came through with the customary "squeeze." T. V. blew up and quit.

But through all political ups and downs he remained head of the Bank of China, ruling one of the world's great financial organizations and providing the international funds to maintain China's fiscal structure; and for the past few years he has served in the government with the rest of his family as foreign minister.

T. V. Soong married Anna Chang, a petite beauty educated in a Christian mission school, who was mistaken for a Chinese movie star when she appeared on the streets of New York wearing, as she always does, a Chinese dress. They have three children.

The Chiangs

I n 1917 Mayling Soong returned to her native land, an honor graduate of Wellesley College and a beauty. During the nine years in America she had improved the time to acquire a culture and self-possession unusual in a miss of her years. She had been all over the country—"in practically every single state," she said—and her use of the English language, including the Georgia accent, was nearly perfect, as American reporters were to discover to their confusion twenty-five years later. She had, of course, become not a little denationalized; for she had left her native land in childhood, and her impressionable years had been spent in a foreign environment, and she thought, dressed, reacted, and looked like an American. Vincent Sheean referred to her as "hyper-Americanized." This she frankly confessed, and it was held against her in China; but what she had gained in education and character, which was permanent, far overbalanced what she had lost of the Chinese spirit, which could be and was regained.

The status of the family had increased since she left. Her father had continued to prosper and had acquired an automobile. Whatever reproach had been attached to his revolutionary activities had been removed by the growing success of that movement. Her mother had become an influential character in church and benevolent circles, and her prestige in these fields was destined to enhance. One of her sisters was married to the nation's most famous man, and the other was the wife of a far-removed son of Confucius whose reputation was already beginning to grow. Mayling of course entered at once the best circles of Shanghai society, especially among the foreigners, the foreign-trained, and those friendly to foreign ways. She wore foreign-style dresses at first, and even hats, and pioneered a new path by appearing in riding breeches. Soon she was in the midst of things. She joined the Y. W. C. A. and was active in its affairs; she was interested in the church; she became a member of the film-censoring committee; she was the first Chinese ever appointed by the municipal authorities as a member of the Child Labor Committee.

But she set about overcoming her "hyper-Americanization" too. She declined all the school-teaching offers that came to her, as they came then to nearly all Chinese with foreign training, and began studying the classics under an old-style scholar. She studied the Chinese language and learned to use it as fluently as she used English. Many returned students did not go to so much trouble. But Mayling Soong was different, and she was determined to reorientalize herself.

It was not long after her return from America that Mayling, visiting her sister at the Sun home in Shanghai, met the young soldier Chiang Kai-shek. It was an encounter to be expected sooner or later, in view of the Soong family's part in the Revolution, for he was a protégé of Dr. Sun, who was already laying plans on the basis of his military skill.

Chiang Kai-shek was just past thirty at the time, having been born October 31, 1887, at Ningpo in the province of Chekiang. His father dying early, he was reared with unusual care by his mother, who was a devout Buddhist and a strict vegetarian. She worshiped every day and devoted especial attention to inculcating religious principles in her son.

"I pray for you," she said to him, "that you should love your country and preserve the good name of your ancestors, who were men of reputation." Chiang attended the village school and then went to the high schools at Fenghuaand Lungchin. His biographer, Hollington K. Tong, says that when he was ten years old an instructor in the local school pointed out the amazing fact that the presidents of the United States considered themselves servants of the people and lived simply. "The president of the United States is a man," retorted the lad, "and there is nothing strange in his living in simple fashion as an ordinary citizen." [1]

In 1906 he entered the Paoting Military Academy and a year later went to Japan to study military science. Here he met the revolutionary leaders Dr. Sun Yat-sen and Chen Chi-mei, espoused the principles of the Revolution, and became a member of the Tungmenghui, the forerunner of the Kuomintang. In 1909 he joined a regiment of the Japanese army in further preparation for the Japanese Military College. Then the Revolution which was to overthrow the Manchus broke out in China. Chiang and other cadets asked two days' leave, slipped away to China, and mailed their swords and uniforms back to regimental headquarters. He took part in the early activities of the revolutionary movement, and when Yuan Shih-kai gained ascendency he accompanied Sun Yat-sen and Charlie Soong in their flight to Japan. It was during these years that he became closely associated with Dr. Sun, who recognized in him not only rare military and political talents but also a passionate devotion to China. During these years also he saw the mounting military power and aggressiveness of Japan and noted it all down for future reference.

---

[1] *Chiang Kai-shek: Soldier and Statesman* (Shanghai: China Publishing Co., 1937), vol. I, pp. 6, 12.

Though he was later to be accused of a policy of appeasement toward China's militant neighbor, he never suffered any disillusionment as to Japan's ultimate intentions.

When, back in China again, Chiang Kai-shek met the little sister of his leader's wife, newly returned from her education in America, he was at once attracted to her; and it was not long before he approached Dr. Sun on the matter of marriage. But the latter was wise in the ways of the Soong family and advised the ardent young soldier to wait. Chiang waited. Then he brought the subject up again, and Sun once more advised him to wait.

If Chiang was disappointed, he was not disheartened. Besides, he had little time for brooding or repining. In 1920 he was appointed head of the Whampoa Military Academy, founded by Dr. Sun Yat-sen on the advice of Michael Borodin, alias Berg, alias Grusenberg, a Russian agent who had been in the United States, Mexico, Scotland, and Turkey on Communist business. The academy was staffed largely by Russian military experts, and its function was to produce a sufficient number of adequately trained officers for the Kuomintang or Nationalist army, which was clearly recognized as necessary if the northern war lords were to be subdued and China welded into a real nation. The cadets were trained in record time, and in six years the Nationalist leaders felt themselves strong enough to try conclusions with the war lords in the field.

Dr. Sun Yat-sen died in March, 1925; and in September Chiang Kai-shek became commander in chief of the forces, which were called the Kuomintangs, Nationalists, Cantonese, or Southerners. The Russian General Galen, alias Bluecher, was his chief of staff. Funds had been made available by the financial policy of T. V. Soong. The first step was to bring the provinces of Kwangtung and Kwangsi entirely under control. Then in 1926 Chiang began his famous northward march, his objective being the Yangtze River and eventually Peking and all China.

The story of the triumphant march of the Kuomintang army under the leadership of Chiang Kai-shek is a classic in recent military history. The provinces submitted one by one as Chiang's army swept everything before it. The Nationalists entered Hankow, Hangchow, Shanghai, and Nanking, gaining control of the strategic areas of the country, and set up a government at Hankow which promised a new order for China.

Then came a series of tragedies. The indiscriminate looting of Nanking by the communistic element in the Nationalist army shook the prestige of the General and led to the expulsion of the Russian element, which had developed strong influence in the Nationalist regime. The Kuomintang was split. The Red group, under the leadership of Eugene Chen, Madame Sun Yat-sen, and the Russians, maintained a government at Hankow, while the more conservative element established a rival government at Nanking. There were minor clashes between the two, with Nanking coming off victorious. Borodin, Chen, Madame Sun, and many other leaders of the Left Wing went to Russia. In spite of the split in his ranks General Chiang Kai-shek continued the drive northward, crossed the Yangtze, and prepared for the final drive on Peking, from which vantage point he expected to drive the Manchurian war lord Chang Tso-lin back into Manchuria and secure the recognition of the foreign powers for his Nationalist government over the whole of China.

He had reached the point, however, where the going had become hard. Between him and Peking was the Russian-drilled army of the "Christian General" Feng Yu-hsiang, with whom Chiang made an alliance and developed plans for a two-pronged drive on Peking. Between Chiang and Peking also lay the province of Shantung, which had been taken by Japan from Germany at the close of the first World War and was filled with Japanese settlers. Chang Tso-lin was suspected of being hand in glove with the Japanese, and the progress of Chiang's armies through Shantung was stoutly resisted by the provincial commanders. At the most critical moment of the war General Feng Yu-hsiang, who now felt that he held the balance of power and therefore the whip hand, took sides with the Red element and demanded that the Nanking government relinquish power in favor of the Hankow radicals. This was a staggering blow to Chiang Kai-shek, and in disgust he announced his resignation as commander in chief of the army and from all official positions in the Kuomintang. He retired to the Hsueh Tou Temple, a beautiful Buddhist monastery in a grove on a mountain in his native province of Chekiang.

That was in August, 1927. The Nationalist cause was at a standstill. Though Hankow was deteriorating, and the Nanking regime was increasing its prestige, the latter was without the military leadership necessary to advance. And so war and politics came to a stalemate while there occurred another event of greater significance for the future of China and of the world.

Through all these stirring scenes in which he was the central figure, the Generalissimo had not abandoned his aim to wed the youngest daughter of Charlie Soong. Having for several years followed Dr. Sun's advice to wait, he determined to approach Mayling herself. She was "not interested." She was devoting herself to work in organizations to improve the lot of the Chinese people—at least a portion of them—and had refused proposals from several young men that seemed more suitable. But Chiang was a persistent suitor. Able to see her but rarely, he kept writing to her; and, as young ladies frequently do, she became more favorably inclined. But she was firm on certain points. There would be no elopement, as in Chingling's case; and there would be no marriage without the consent of Madame Soong. That raised a difficulty, for the family was opposed to the match. Madame Sun Yat-sen declared she "would rather see her little sister dead" than the wife of Chiang. Her mother's opposition was deeply based on religious scruples and was more serious than her objection to Chingling's marriage to Dr. Sun. The latter was at least a Christian; but the General was a Buddhist, he had a wife and two sons living, and malicious tongues had spread gossip about him.

In the marriage of each of their daughters the Soongs ran up against the conflict between Christian ethics and non-Christian practices, since the three men involved had been married in the customary boy-and-girl affairs arranged by the families. In Eling's case there was no problem, because Dr. Kung's wife was dead. Chingling took her case out of the family hands. But now the issue had to be faced.

Chiang's marriage had been arranged by his mother when he was only fifteen years old, and for years the General had seen little of his wife. Hollington Tong says she had

many admirable qualities, not least among them generosity as she showed later, but she was in no sense politically minded, and it was difficult for her to realize the intense devotion to the revolutionary cause that Chiang developed almost as soon as he could think. . . . . She found it difficult to reconcile herself to the prolonged absences of her husband, and repeatedly urged him to abandon his political and military activities. Naturally advice of this kind was not acceptable to a young man who was almost fanatical in his enthusiasm for the revolutionary cause, for which he was ready to sacrifice his life. . . . . Eventually his wife recognized that she was really a hindrance to Chiang, or rather to the career upon which he had embarked, and by an amicable arrangement a divorce on the ground of incompatibility was obtained and registered. Undoubtedly the wife was grieved, but she had the intuition and generosity to realize that national were more powerful than domestic claims.[2]

Tong declares that this was twelve months before the General had met Mayling Soong.

But the religious issue remained. No non-Christian should marry into the family if Madame Soong could prevent it. She persistently refused to see Chiang, which in itself would have been sufficient answer to most persons conversant with Chinese etiquette, but it did not discourage him. He pressed his suit; Madame Soong went to Japan; Chiang followed. When finally she was persuaded to grant an interview, the General made clear the fact that he had satisfactorily adjusted his domestic affairs, and Madame Soong bluntly asked him if he would become a Christian. He replied that his understanding was that a real Christian is one who has a personal experience of God, and so he would not profess conversion as part of a matrimonial bargain; but he would study Christianity, read the Bible with an open mind, and pray sincerely for divine guidance to a right decision. No answer could have pleased Madame Soong more, since it bespoke the honesty of the man, and she believed that any person who would read the Bible and pray would certainly be led by the Holy Spirit into an experience of Christian faith.

When Madame Soong's consent had been secured, another difficulty presented itself. The mother wanted her daughter, the daughter of Charlie Soong, circuit rider, to be married in their church and by their own pastor. She had been denied this joy in the cases of the other girls, but she had become

[2] *Chiang Kai-shek,* vol. I, pp. 185-86.

more of a saint in the meantime and now desired it very much. Unfortunately for all concerned, the Methodist *Discipline* declared: "The ministers of our Church shall be prohibited from solemnizing the rites of matrimony between divorced persons, except in case of innocent parties who have been divorced for the one scriptural cause"—namely, adultery, which did not enter into the Chiang divorce. Bishop Ainsworth was in China, and he dearly loved the little girl who had played about his home with his daughter in America; but church law is especially binding on bishops, and he was out of the question. So they turned to the Soong pastor, the Rev. Z. T. Kaung, then minister of the Young J. Allen Memorial Church, and now a bishop himself.

But Pastor Kaung declined also, in spite of the close relations between him and the family, his respect for the leader of the nation, his hope of winning the General for the Christian faith, and the natural desire of any minister to serve in such a distinguished capacity. Next to his faith and goodness, Pastor Kaung was noted for his love and loyalty to his church. He could not perform the rites.

Those who claim to know something about the circumstances aver that Madame Soong argued the point:

The General's marriage was an arranged Buddhist affair and not a Christian alliance; he had set matters right; in everything he had lived up to the light he had!

True enough, and it was not on the General's account that the pastor hesitated, nor did he pass censure on the General! What about Mayling? She was no Buddhist; she knew the Christian ethics!

Would Pastor Kaung perform a second and private ceremony?

Sorry, but he could not.

Would he come to the house and pray with the couple? He would.

And in Madame Soong's house Pastor Kaung, Madame Soong, Mayling, and Generalissimo Chiang Kai-shek knelt together while the pastor prayed for the blessing and guidance of God forever to attend the couple.

The wedding occurred on the first day of December, 1927. It was a great affair in Shanghai when the daughter of the noted house of Soong married the powerful former leader of the Chinese armies. There were two weddings, a quiet Christian ceremony at home performed by Dr. David Yui, well-known national secretary of the Y.M.C.A. in China, followed by the brilliant official Chinese rites at the swanky Majestic Hotel. All the dignitaries and socially elite of the city were there. The ritual was elaborate, in ten parts, and was conducted by the minister of education, a former president of the Peking National University, Dr. Tsai Yuan-pei. The bride and groom posed for the movie cameras, bowed three times before the portrait of Dr. Sun Yat-sen and the flags of China and the Kuomintang, heard the reading of the marriage certificate and saw the official seal placed on it, bowed to each other, bowed to the witnesses, and bowed to the guests. Then they sat in two chairs under a great floral bell, and somebody pulled a ribbon and released a shower of rose petals on them. There were American touches too: a tenor sang "O Promise Me," and the newspapers described the dresses worn by the women.

The pageantry in the luxurious Majestic Hotel gave little presage of what was in store for the bride. The Nationalist government straightway begged Chiang to come back, and when General Feng promised to support him he consented. Their week-old honeymoon interrupted, the pair set out for Nanking. It was then that Madame Chiang began to learn how little, despite all her studies, she knew about the real China, for she had previously seen only the comparatively modernized coastal cities. Nanking, still early in the process of being made into a modern capital, was a mixture of ancient ruins and new ugliness, with all the dirt, crowding, and squalor which Madame Chiang has since done so much to reduce throughout the country. Most of the wives of officials refused to live there and stayed in Shanghai or other more comfortable spots, but Charlie Soong's daughter set values above comfort. When after a winter of preparation her husband took the field with the avowed purpose of suppressing the Communists, she went with him. Through the months and years of civil war that followed she stayed by his side, under conditions that made Nanking seem the height of luxury. Chiang fought the Communists and war lords everywhere, with varying fortunes, laboring at the same time to consolidate a government which would truly represent the Kuomintang and the Three Principles enunciated by Sun Yat-sen. In July, 1928, the Nationalist armies triumphantly entered Peking. In December the "Young Marshal" Chang Hsueh-liang, son of old Chang Tso-lin, announced his adherence to Nanking and accepted a place on the National State Council; and the Nationalist flag was raised over Mukden, the capital of Manchuria. In theory, at least, China was unified under one central government, but there were still armies under the radical leaders antagonistic to Chiang and Nanking to be subdued—a task to keep the Generalissimo busy until a more formidable threat against China was to appear from the outside.

Meanwhile, Chiang Kai-shek was keeping his promise to Madame Soong—to study the Bible, pray, and follow the light and leading vouchsafed to him. The Generalissimo was and is a very sincere man, and an abiding interest in spiritual things had been deeply planted in him by his Buddhist mother. Furthermore, he had a profound respect for Madame Soong, who exercised a strong influence over him. Faithfully he read the Bible which she had given him, concentrating first on the Old Testament. When his wife prayed at night, he knelt with her. He prayed himself and sought guidance. But the search of a soul for God is not always easy, and in the case of the Generalissimo it involved struggle. His background was alien to the Christian gospel, and the "apperceptive mass" of training was absent. He was uninstructed, and the Old Testament is a difficult book—difficult to read and still more difficult to understand and appropriate. His progress was slow.

One was ever near him, however, to encourage and guide, though, as she has declared, she was still at an early stage of spiritual growth herself. Madame Chiang prayed with him and tried to answer his questions and, consciously or unconsciously, kept strong upon him the influence of her mother. Once the Generalissimo asked her, "What, exactly, is a Christian?" and she replied, "My mother is the finished product. I am a Christian in the making."

Another helper there was in the person of the Soong pastor, Dr. Kaung, who had feared that he was forfeiting the friendship of the family when he declined to officiate at the wedding, but found on the contrary that his adherence to conscience and duty had won the deep respect of the Generalissimo and opened up the opportunity to give him spiritual guidance as well as Biblical enlightenment.

One day in 1928 Pastor Kaung received a telegram from Madame Chiang summoning him to Nanking. She believed the Generalissimo was "not far from the Kingdom" and wanted the minister to talk with him—perhaps to persuade him. To escape the confusion of state affairs they took an automobile ride about the city, and the pastor sat between the pair and talked religion to the Generalissimo. But Chiang was not to be hurried; he declared he did not yet know enough about Christianity to seek baptism; he had only completed the reading of the Old Testament and was beginning the New. But Pastor Kaung was leaving for America, Madame pointed out. The pastor agreed with the General and would not urge him; clearly he was not ready.

Dr. Kaung later told the interesting story of what occurred while he was in America. It appears that in a local war between the Central Government and recalcitrant elements the Generalissimo was trapped and surrounded near Kaifeng, and capture and death appeared imminent. There was a little country church near his headquarters, and Chiang entered it to pray. There he made a vow to become a follower of Christ if he survived. Said Dr. Kaung:

His prayers were answered; a heavy snowstorm broke and held up his enemies' advance, and reinforcements arrived two days later. Thus his life was not only saved but an apparent defeat had been turned into victory. Then it was that he made up his mind to accept Christ. When I returned from America, I was asked to baptize the leader of China into the membership of the Christian Church.

Chiang was baptized by Pastor Kaung on October 23, 1930, in the room in Madame Soong's home where the pastor prayed with and for the couple before their wedding. A few friends, missionaries and Chinese, were present, and of course the family—including Madame Soong, in failing health and with only nine months to live. When the time came for the vows of church membership, Madame Chiang rose quietly and walked from her place in the corner of the room to stand beside her husband; and as he spoke in answer to the pastor's questions, she softly but firmly said the words with him, re-dedicating herself. After the ritual, all rose and sang together the hymn:

> O happy day, that fixed my choice
> On Thee, my Saviour and my God!

When the news of Chiang's conversion and baptism was flashed around the world, cynical speculation as to reasons and motives began. There were editorials about currying favor with America and Britain and seeking foreign support in the coming struggle with Japan. But one editor rebuked his colleagues: "Does it not occur to you that he might have had an experience of God in his heart?" Such is the import of the only answer the Generalissimo himself gave when asked the reason for his step: "I feel the need of a God such as Jesus Christ"—which is, as another American editor commented, "a great confession. A theologian with hours of study could not frame a better or more significant." Many who knew Chiang then vouched for his sincerity, and few would doubt it now.

The factors leading to a decision of such significance, involving a decisive break with the ancient traditions of the nation over which he ruled, cannot be segregated and identified one by one. His promise to Madame Soong, his love for his wife, his study of the Bible all entered into it. The influence of his Christian colleagues in the government had been great. Writing several months before the Generalissimo's decision, Bishop W. N. Ainsworth, friend of the family since Wesleyan days, said:

There are ten secretaries or department heads, constituting the cabinet of President Chiang Kai-shek, and seven of the ten are Christian men. The president himself is not a Christian, but

in a lengthy interview he told me that he had marked the differ-
ence between his Christian associates and the politicians of the
old type. His brilliant wife spoke to me over and over of her
own faith in Jesus Christ and the inspiration of her student days
in America, when she resided in my house. She expressed the
assurance that God would yet bring her husband with her into
the fellowship of the Christian faith.[3]

Chiang's biographer, Hollington K. Tong, is of the opinion
that the Generalissimo was "leading a Christian life con-
sistently even before his formal conversion to that faith,"
and he quotes the words of one who accompanied him during
the war in Honan:

Judging from his daily life one cannot but admit that long ago
he was a Christian in spirit. . . . . While at the front, even when
under artillery fire, one could always see this copy of the Bible
on his desk, besides files of official papers. What was more praise-
worthy, General Chiang not only kept the Bible, but read it regularly. Long before he was baptized he had already acquired
the habit of praying at length.[4]

He believes also that the Generalissimo has continued to
grow spiritually:

He reads the Bible several times a day, and is a genuinely zealous Christian. The public does not realize the important influence
exerted by Christianity upon the Generalissimo's character and
official career since his conversion shortly after his marriage.
Those closest to the Generalissimo Chiang and his wife make no
secret of the fact that for the last few years they kneel together
and pray jointly every morning and evening, imploring wisdom
and justice for the conduct of their personal and official affairs.
Grace precedes their meals. This deep piety is recognized and
respected by all members of the Government, even those who are

---

[3] "The Mountain Moves," *The Missionary Voice*, April, 1930, pp. 152-53.
[4] Tong, *Chiang Kai-shek*, vol. II, p. 595.

still Buddhists or Confucianists, or who belong to other faiths. Careful observers of his career note a marked change in Chiang's methods and policies since his adoption of Christianity. In earlier years, he believed in the use of force, but latterly has strongly favoured conciliation and the avoidance of bloodshed, and has become more emphatic in his denunciation of venality and corruption in public life. His piety has reached the point where he always carries with him on his train and airplane journeys the copy of the Bible given to him by the late Madame Soong, his mother-in-law.[5]

That Madame Chiang has grown by her husband's influence no less than he by hers is revealed by what she has written:

And then I realized that spiritually I was failing my husband. My mother's influence on the General had been tremendous. His own mother was a devout Buddhist. It was *my* mother's influence and personal example that led him to become a Christian. Too honest to promise to be one just to win her consent to our marriage, he had promised my mother that he would study Christianity and read the Bible. And I suddenly realized that he was sticking to his promise, even after she was gone, but losing spiritually because there were so many things he did not understand. . . . .

I began to see that what I was doing to help, for the sake of the country, was only a substitute for what he needed. I was letting him head toward a mirage when I knew of the oasis. Life was all confusion. I had been in the depths of despair. Out of that, and the feeling of human inadequacy, I was driven back to my mother's God. I knew there was a power greater than myself. I knew God was there. But Mother was no longer there to do my interceding for me. It seemed to be up to me to help the General spiritually, and in helping him I grew spiritually myself.[6]

---

[5] *Ibid.*, vol. II, pp. 481-82.
[6] "What Religion Means to Me," *Forum,* March, 1934, p. 132.

The leader of China's millions and the daughter of Charlie Soong have climbed the golden ladder of faith together.

The most significant sequel to the Generalissimo's adoption of Christianity for himself has been the inauguration of the New Life Movement for his country—an ambitious moral and ethical enterprise which proposed nothing less than a Chinese renaissance, a complete reformation of the habits, customs, and manners of one fourth of the whole human race, to bring them more in line with the accepted morals of Christian civilization. According to Mr. Tong's biography, written in 1937, Chiang believed then—and perhaps still believes—that the future would find his chief claim to the gratitude of his people not in his military achievements but in this movement. At any rate, it is probable that no other military man in all history has ever thrown so much into a movement of such a messianic character. Nobody could have conceived it save one whose interests lay far deeper than the ordinary matters of politics and government.

The need for a "reformation of manners" flashed on the spiritually alert conscience of the Generalissimo one day in 1934 when he saw small boys indulging in unseemly behavior on the public streets. The spark found abundant tinder in Madame Chiang's strong social consciousness—planted, she herself suggests, by her contact with hill-country classmates in the eighth grade in Georgia, but more recently forced to maturity by constant observation of the great needs of her people while accompanying the Generalissimo on his military campaigns. She helped him lay the plans and then became the movement's directing genius, though he remained its honorary chief.

Because of its insistence upon certain rules of dress and personal conduct, the New Life Movement was at first ridiculed by the cynical; and even the scholarly Dr. Hu Shih criticized it on the ground that it was too spiritual and idealistic, whereas "the basis of living is economic and material." As a matter of fact its principles plumb the depths of Chinese character. Foreigners have never been able to understand the general carelessness and backwardness of China, in view of the nation's long history and invaluable artistic and cultural contributions. Filthy cities, the opium habit, addiction to gambling, incompetence and graft in official life, the callousness of the upper classes toward the poor and suffering, the lack of a real national consciousness as evidenced by the prevalence of civil wars and the ease with which they are promoted—these, indeed, are not exclusively Chinese, but in China they were certainly prevalent enough to provoke the wonder of the rest of the world. The New Life Movement, as conceived by Generalissimo and Madame Chiang, struck at the roots of these things in the hearts of the people. It resurrected four ancient Chinese virtues: *li,* or right mental and spiritual attitudes; *i,* or right conduct; *lien,* or discrimination and honesty in personal and official life; and *chih,* or integrity and honor. In matters of conduct it laid down eight principles:

1. Regard yesterday as a period of death, today as a period of life. Let us rid ourselves of old abuses and build up a new nation.

2. Let us accept the heavy responsibilities of reviving the nation.

3. We must observe rules and have faith, honesty, and shame.

4. Our clothing, eating, living, and traveling must be simple, orderly, plain, and clean.

5. We must willingly face hardships. We must strive for frugality.

6. We must have adequate knowledge and moral integrity as citizens.

7. Our actions must be courageous and rapid.

8. We must act on our promises, or even act without promising.

In launching the New Life Movement one of the first steps was to confer with and seek the aid of the Christian missionaries of all denominations. In various places the Generalissimo invited all the missionaries to meet him and Maddame Chiang, informing them that the Nationalist government endorsed their work and welcomed their co-operation in the uplift of the masses. The missionaries generally accepted his invitation to forward the New Life Movement, and more and more it took on the character of a Christian program. It was organized in all the provinces; its meetings were attended by huge throngs; and most of the men and women prominent in public life gave it their support. Antiopium campaigns were projected and clinics established; laws were enacted providing for the cure of opium addicts; and drastic penalties, including confiscation of property and death, were imposed for the use—after clinical treatment—and sale of the drug. A complementary movement was launched for the preservation of ancient Chinese relics. By the time the all-out aggression of Japan necessitated redirection of the program to war needs, a hundred thousand workers had been enlisted, and noticeable gains had been made in the orderliness, cleanliness, and general morale of the people.

The Tiger's Lair

SHORTLY after the nation had celebrated the fiftieth birthday of the Generalissimo—in 1936, for Chinese are one year old when they are born—there occurred a bewildering event that aroused all China and startled the world. It was so strange that many persons could not at the time believe in its reality, and there were insinuations that it was a performance planned with an eye on Chinese morale.

Chiang Kai-shek was in a tight place during that period. The anti-Red campaigns had not gone well. The Japanese were constantly increasing their encroachments, and everybody knew that outright and total war was inevitable. In 1931 they had invaded Manchuria and in February of the following year set up a puppet state there called Manchukuo with the dethroned Manchu dynast Henry Pu Yi as emperor. Not content with detaching this vast area from China, they had taken the province of Jehol and advanced within the Great Wall. Then they had occupied Chapei, in the native section of Shanghai, and destroyed a large part of the city. In spite of these military operations, however, war was not officially declared. China was not ready to fight; and Chiang was temporizing to gain time for more adequate preparation, the enlistment of foreign sympathy and support, and the unification of all Chinese factions to oppose the common enemy.

As the Japanese took more and more Chinese territory without meeting serious armed resistance, they became more arrogant and constantly increased their demands. School-books must be censored and all references unfavorable to Japan eliminated; newspapers must be restricted in their utterances; persons so unfortunate as to incur Japanese dis-pleasure must be imprisoned; boycott of Japanese goods must be prohibited; the Kuomintang itself must be dissolved. Chiang made gestures in all such cases, and thereby drew down on his head the censure of a considerable section of the Chinese press and public which did not understand his policy or the necessity for it. Indeed, dissatisfaction found open expression in a small revolution in the South when Chiang Kai-shek did not obey the telegraphed advice of mili-tary leaders there and embark on all-out war against Japan. In the North the same motive actuated two of his own generals, Yang Hu-cheng and the "Young Marshal" Chang Hsueh-liang. The Young Marshal had ample cause to hate and fight the Japanese; they had taken from him the whole of his province of Manchuria, and it was generally accepted that they had planted the bomb which killed his father, Chang Tso-lin.

The story has been told in Chiang's *Diary*, in Madame Chiang's *Sian, a Coup d'État*, and in the various published histories and biographies dealing with modern China and the Chinese; and the details are familiar. The Generalissimo had gone to the province of Shensi for conferences with his gen-erals there. He was aroused by the sound of gunfire on the morning of December 12 and found his headquarters sur-rounded by recalcitrant troops of Chang's army. He suf-fered some injuries in attempting to escape and then came boldly forward and announced his identity. He was taken to Sian and placed in detention in the New City Building, or the Pacification Commissioner's Headquarters, occupied by Yang, later being transferred to safer and more comfortable quarters. Here he faced the Young Marshal and heard the arguments and demands of his captors for certain reforms in the government and a firmer attitude toward Japan.

Chiang Kai-shek stood firm, not only against the demands but even against discussing such matters with his subordinates under duress. "Since you call me Generalissimo," he said to Chang, "then you are my subordinate. Today you can treat me only in one of two ways. If you recognize me as your superior officer, you should immediately escort me back to Loyang; otherwise you are a rebel. If I am in rebel hands, then you can immediately kill me. Besides this there is nothing more to be said." That was his consistent attitude during the two weeks of his captivity. He was ready to die but not to yield position or principle under constraint.

"Why do you insist upon sacrificing yourself for the sake of principles and not think of the possibility of achievements?" asked Chang. "I think you are the only great man of this age, but why won't you yield a little, comply with our requests, and lead us on in the Revolution so that we may achieve something instead of merely sacrificing your life? In our opinion, to sacrifice one's life is certainly not a good plan, nor the real object of a revolutionary."

To this the Generalissimo made a notable reply: "If I should try to save my life today and forget the welfare of the nation and the question of life and death of the race, or if I become afraid in the face of danger, my character as a military man will be destroyed, and the nation will be in a precarious position. This means that the nation will perish when I live. On the other hand, if I stand firm and would rather sacrifice my life than compromise my principles, I shall be able to maintain my integrity till death, and my spirit will live forever. Then multitudes of others will follow me, and bear the duties of office according to this spirit of sacrifice. Then, though I die, the nation will live. So if anyone wrongly thinks that he can manipulate national affairs by capturing me and endangering my life, he is a perfect fool."

The Young Marshal telegraphed the Nanking government that he assumed responsibility for the personal safety of the Generalissimo whom he gave assurance should not be injured. He wired to Dr. Kung: "I love the Generalissimo as much today as eight years ago. I assume full responsibility for his safety and will not allow any injury to be done to him." And to Madame Chiang: "All my life I have not once proved myself ungrateful. I can swear this before Heaven. Please do not feel anxious about the Generalissimo."

Chang made eight demands of the government, including release of all political offenders, cessation of civil war, admission of all parties and elements to the government, and repeal of all restrictions on liberty of assembly. To the British press agency he explained his actions and purposes thus:

An active anti-Japanese struggle is the only way out for China, which is unanimously demanded by the people. To realize this, we continually offered advice, which was firmly rejected by the Generalissimo. We are thus compelled to keep him here to give him the last chance of awakening. As soon as the Generalissimo gives up his fallacious policy and mobilizes an active anti-Japanese struggle, we shall immediately become his loyal followers again and will fight on the first front. Our real purpose is purely for national salvation and there is absolutely nothing personal. This is not a mutiny at all, but a necessary step of really consolidating all the political parties in the country to shoulder the responsibility of national salvation. The Generalissimo is in perfectly good condition and well treated here.

In the meantime all China was in an uproar. Rumors of all kinds flew about. Prayers were offered in all the churches and in the non-Christian temples. Great tension prevailed in official circles at Nanking. The government refused to treat with Chang Hsueh-liang and prepared for a military drive on Sian by air and land. W. H. Donald, Australian friend and adviser to both Chiang and Chang; Colonel J. L. Huang, bulky Vanderbilt graduate who was general secretary of the New Life Movement; T. V. Soong; and others flew to Sian and negotiated with the captors in unofficial capacities. The Generalissimo himself read his Bible and reflected upon the attitude of Jesus in such a crisis.

It was the reading of Chiang's carefully kept diary and the official papers and personal letters seized, as much as anything else, that influenced his captors in his favor and prepared the way for the final negotiations. Until they had seen these documents they did not understand the real nature and policy of the man with whom they were dealing. "We have read your diary and other important documents," Chang told him, "and from them have learned the greatness of your personality; your loyalty to the revolutionary cause and your determination to bear the responsibility of saving the country far exceed anything we could have imagined. You have blamed me in your diary for having no character. I now really feel that this may be so. Your great fault is that you have always spoken too little of your mind to your subordinates. If I had known one tenth of what is recorded in your diary, I would certainly not have done this rash act. Now I know very clearly that my former views were wrong."

The Generalissimo wrote a letter to Madame Chiang and read it aloud several times to Colonel Huang, to whom it was entrusted, because "letters sometimes get lost." This one did; it was taken away from Huang the moment he left the room, and Huang himself was imprisoned. The letter said:

As I have made up my mind to sacrifice my life, if necessary, for my country, please do not worry about me. I will never allow myself to do anything to make my wife ashamed of me, or become unworthy of being a follower of Dr. Sun Yat-sen. Since I was born for the Revolution, I will gladly die for the same cause. I will return my body unspotted to my parents. As to home affairs, I have nothing to say further than that I wish you would, to gladden my spirit, regard my two sons, Ching-kuo and Wei-kuo, as your own children. However, you must never come to Shensi.

But Madame Chiang did go to Shensi. Told the news by Dr. Kung in Shanghai, she had rushed at once to Nanking. The military-minded there were determined to crush the revolt at once, regardless of the danger to their leader, lest the prestige of the government be destroyed. When she spoke in opposition, they discounted her words as the pleadings of a wife for the life of her husband; but they found it hard to deny her argument that only the Generalissimo could save China from a disastrous civil war which would lay the country at the mercy of Japan. Her courage, self-control, and sound judgment won out—and no doubt saved both her husband and her country. The Nationalist armies drew in around the "rebel stronghold" but did not attack. Then after ten days of negotiations by the emissaries had failed to secure the Generalissimo's release, Madame Chiang herself boarded a plane at Nanking and, disregarding all warnings of the danger, flew to Sian. As she came down over the city, she handed a revolver to W. H. Donald, who accompanied her, and instructed him to shoot her if she was seized by the hostile troops on landing. Donald took the gun and promised to obey instructions, but he later declared he had no intention of actually doing so.

Press Association, Inc.

THE GENERAL FIGHTS, WOOS, AND WEDS

In the Nationalist uniform; on a "date" at the Kung home in Shanghai;
at the Majestic Hotel, Shanghai, December, 1927

International Newsreel

Press Association, Inc.

THE CHIANGS AT NANKING

When the New Life Movement was occupying most of their attention

Chang Hsueh-liang met her at the airport, and as if nothing had occurred to interrupt their good relationships she shook hands with him and went at once to drink tea with him and his fellow conspirator, Yang Hu-cheng. When she was escorted to her husband's quarters, Chiang cried out, "Why have you come? You have walked into a tiger's lair."

"I have come to see you," she answered quietly and simply. Later he wrote in his diary, "I was very much moved and wanted to cry."

Then the Generalissimo admitted that he knew she was coming to save him, for that very day he had read in the thirty-first chapter of Jeremiah: "Jehovah hath created a new thing in the earth: A woman shall encompass [protect] a man."

"I noticed," she wrote in her own account, "that his recital of what he had suffered on the morning of December 12 upset him emotionally and agitated his mind. To calm him I opened the Psalms and read to him until he drifted off to quiet sleep."

The woman really did "encompass a man." For two days she and her brother T. V. talked with the two rebellious generals. Soon the Young Marshal was pleading with her: "Please, you try to make the Generalissimo less angry and tell him we really do not want anything, not even for him to sign anything. We do not want money, nor do we want territory." Chang was won over, but Yang held out, on the ground that Madame and T. V. would protect the former while Yang himself had no prospect of security. "T. V. is very much upset," ran the Generalissimo's diary, "but I am taking it quite calmly, as I have not been expecting to leave this dangerous place. The question of life and death bothers me no more." However much T. V.'s sister was upset, she maintained her poise before the captors; and on Christmas Day the doors swung open, and the Generalissimo was set free. The Young

Marshal even insisted on escorting him personally to Nanking. It was a glad and noisy day throughout all China.

After his release had been decided upon and before he left Sian, the Generalissimo called Chang Hsueh-liang and Yang Hu-cheng to him and addressed them on the seriousness of their action. He pointed out that since they were ready to correct their mistake and had acknowledged his sincerity in the conduct of the war they would be entitled to remain as his subordinates. Since assuming command, he declared, he had acted upon and inculcated in his subordinates two principles: "(1) If I have any selfish motives or do anything against the welfare of the country and the people, then anybody may consider me a traitor and may shoot me on that account. (2) If my words and deeds are in the least insincere and I neglect the principles and revolutionary ideals, my soldiers may treat me as their enemy and may also shoot me."

Chiang declared that while he recognized that the recalcitrants had been deceived by propaganda, which had been proved false by the reading of his diary and letters, the responsibility for their action rested upon them and they must submit to the authority of the Central Government. At the same time he said he took a degree of the blame on himself, since he had been careless about his own personal safety and the discipline of the army, and as commander in chief he must bear at least a part of the responsibility for the actions of his subordinates. Therefore he also would submit to the Central Government and ask the authorities to punish him. In view of their repentance and willingness to correct the mistake he would intercede to the authorities on their behalf, and he believed leniency would be extended to them.

I have always impressed upon the people the importance of ethical principles and integrity in order to cultivate a sense of probity and of shame, to bear responsibility and to obey discipline. If a superior officer cannot make his subordinates observe these principles, he himself is partly to be blamed. Hence, in connection with this crisis, I am ready to bear the responsibility as your superior officer. On your part, you should be ready to abide by whatever decision the Central Government may make, and your subordinates need not have any fear for themselves.

We must always remember that the life of the nation is more important than anything else. We should not care for ourselves, although our personal integrity must be preserved in order that the nation may exist on a firm foundation. Our lives may be sacrificed, but the law and discipline of the nation must be upheld. Our bodies may be confined, but our spirit must be free. My own responsibility to the country and the Central Government will always be willingly borne as long as I live. That is why I have repeatedly refused to give any orders or sign anything you wanted me to sign while under duress. It is because I consider life or death a small matter compared with the upholding of moral principles.

My words are not only to be left to posterity, but I want you to understand them so that you will also value moral principles more than anything else. I have said more than once that, if I should make any promise to you or sign anything at your request while at Sian, it would amount to the destruction of the nation. If I should try to avoid danger and submit to any duress exercised by my subordinates, my own integrity would be destroyed, and with it the integrity of the nation, which I represent. No matter whether it be an individual or a nation, the loss of integrity is tantamount to death itself. For the upholding of these moral principles which I have repeatedly emphasized to the people, I am ready to undergo any sacrifice. If I do not carry out my own teachings, my subordinates as well as the people of the country will not know what to follow and the nation will be as good as destroyed.

On December 26 the strangely assorted group reached Nanking: the Generalissimo and Madame Chiang Kai-shek and the "rebel" kidnaper Chang Hsueh-liang, who was lodged in the home of T. V. Soong and later in the home of H. H. Kung, both friends of long standing. Then followed a series of events which probably could never have occurred outside of China. The Young Marshal took all the blame upon himself, offered no defense, and begged for punishment. He wrote a letter of apology to Chiang Kai-shek:

I am by nature rustic, surly and unpolished, due to which I have created an incident, which was at once impudent and law-breaking. I have committed a great crime. I have shamefacedly followed you to Nanking in order sincerely to await my punishment by you, punishment befitting in severity the degree of my crime, so that it may not only uphold law and discipline, but also serve as a warning to others in future against repetitions of such a crime. Whatever is beneficial to our country, I shall never decline, even if it means death. I beg you to leave aside sentiments of personal friendship, and let nothing hold you back from giving me the kind of punishment I deserve.

On the other hand, the Generalissimo accepted the blame, declared the unhappy occurrence was due to his own carelessness and that as the superior officer he was responsible for the acts of his subordinates, and asked for the pardon of his abductor. He resigned all his offices in army and government—he offered three resignations, but none was accepted. Chiang wrote:

I believe that the State should uphold its discipline. Only then could one's responsibility be established. Since I was ignorant of such a mutiny brewing and had failed to check it at its outbreak, which resulted in my subordinates taking such rash steps, I had not lived up to the sacred charge thrust upon me. There is, therefore, more reason why I should not stave off the responsibility. I sincerely hope that the Central Executive Committee will censure me for my negligence of duties. During recent years, both my health and my mind have failed me and I have committed many errors in discharging my duties. I should not have shouldered such a heavy load of responsibilities in the first place. After the Sian incident, I am conscience-stricken and it is no longer fit for me to continue in office. I therefore respectfully request the Central Executive Committee to accept my resignation from the posts of President of the Executive Yuan and concurrently Chairman of the National Military Council. I further request the Central Executive Committee immediately to appoint some other competent men to take over my duties, so I may retire from active service and await disciplinary punishment.

The Young Marshal was tried by a special court of the National Military Council. He offered no defense and was sentenced to ten years imprisonment and the deprivation of civil rights for five years. At once the Generalissimo interposed a plea for clemency. "After several delicate readjustments," as Chiang wrote to Yang, who was allowed to retain his command but was a source of future trouble, Chang was "granted a special pardon" but "placed under surveillance," and shortly thereafter his civil rights were restored.

Tongues wagged again. What kind of a deal had been made with the rebels? Had a general ever before begged free pardon for rebels against his own person? Chiang was known as a hard man, and he held the power of life and death; hence there was something behind the scene in this brotherly forgiveness!

There was indeed something behind it—Madame Soong's Bible and General Chiang's faith. In an amazing public statement on Good Friday, March 26, 1937, the Generalissimo told the story of his spiritual life during his captivity:

I have now been a Christian for nearly ten years and during that time I have been a constant reader of the Bible. Never before has this sacred book been so interesting to me as during my two weeks' captivity in Sian. This unfortunate affair took place all of a sudden and I found myself placed under detention without having a single earthly belonging. From my captors I asked but one thing, a copy of the Bible. In my solitude I had ample opportunity for reading and meditation. The greatness and love of Christ burst upon me with new inspiration, increasing my strength to struggle against evil, to overcome temptation and to uphold righteousness. . . . .

The many virtues of Christ I cannot possibly enumerate. To-day being Good Friday, I merely wish to explain some of the lessons I have derived from the trials of Christ. His utterances from the Cross are our spiritual inheritance. Entreating forgiveness for his enemies, he cried: "Father, forgive them: for they know not what they do." Truly great is the love of Christ! In all my meditations I found these thoughts recurring and providing me with rich spiritual sustenance.

To illustrate, I am going to recount some of my experiences at Sian. Before I went to Shensi on my second trip I was already conscious of perverted thoughts and unusual activities in the army there. I had previously received reports of intrigues and revolutionary rumblings that were threatening to undermine the unity of the State. My immediate associates tried to persuade me to abandon the journey, but I replied: "Now that our country is unified and the foundations of the State established, the commander-in-chief of the armies has responsibilities for direction and enlightenment from which he dare not withdraw. Furthermore, I have dedicated my soul and body to the service of the State, and there can never be any consideration of my personal safety."

According to the record of the New Testament, when Christ entered Jerusalem for the last time, he plainly knew that danger was ahead, but triumphantly, on an ass, he rode into the city without anguish, without fears. What greatness! What courage!

In comparison, how unimportant my life must be. So why should I hesitate?

My fondness for my troops has always been as great as the love between brothers, and this love drew me into the heart of the rebellion. Such disregard of danger in the face of duty caused deep concern to the government, worried the people, and, for this, numerous prayers were offered by Christian friends. In the midst of it all my understanding increased and my love multiplied.

Following my detention my captors presented me with terms and demands, with tempting words of kindnesses, with threats of violence and torture and with a public trial by the "People's Front." On every hand I was beset by danger, but I had no thought of yielding to pressure. My faith in Christ increased. In this strange predicament I distinctly recalled the forty days and nights Christ passed in the wilderness withstanding temptation, his prayers in the garden of Gethsemane, and the indignities heaped upon him at his trial. The prayers he offered for his enemies upon the cross were ever in my thoughts. I naturally remembered the prayers offered by Dr. Sun Yat-sen during his imprisonment in London. These scenes passed vividly before me again and again like so many pictures. My strength was redoubled to resist the recalcitrants, and with the spirit of Christ on the cross I was preparing to make the final sacrifice at the trial of the so-called "People's Front." Having determined upon this course of action, I was comforted and at rest.

Following the settlement of the Sian affair, the rebels, knowing their unwise and treasonable actions, were naturally afraid. Remembering that Christ enjoined us to forgive those who sin against us until seventy times seven and upon their repentance, I felt that they should be allowed to start life anew! At the same time I was greatly humbled that my own faith had not been of such quality as to influence my followers and to restrain them.

In July of 1937 the military rulers in Tokyo, realizing that Chiang's temporizing policy was but preparation for the day when he could drive them from Chinese territory and crush their imperial aspirations, began their full-scale undeclared war. Subsequent events are of course well known. Chiang was able immediately to unite all Chinese forces against the aggressor. No match for the highly industrialized Japanese in equipment, he played a masterful game of trading space for time. Though soon driven back from the coastal areas, he transferred his headquarters from Nanking westward in turn to Hankow, Changsha, and—at the end of 1938—Chungking; and in the years since he has held the Japanese practically at the same line. After the sneak attack on Pearl Harbor of December 7, 1941, brought the United States, Britain, and their allies into the conflict in the Orient, China became one of the United Nations, and Generalissimo Chiang Kai-shek the supreme commander of Allied land and air forces in the Chinese theater of the global war.

The answer to aggression has shown the world Madame Chiang's true greatness no less than her husband's. Co-leader of the Chinese nation in fact, if not in name, she shares the dangers on the fighting front and sits in the official councils of the government; she inspires, advises, leads, and bears the burdens of the embattled people—not alone as the wife of the Generalissimo, but in her own right. She is a lieutenant colonel in the Chinese Air Force and for a time was its commander; and she was honorary commander of the Flying Tigers, American air aces fighting for China. Her work for the war orphans of China—her famous "Warphans"—is known everywhere, and she has received large sums of money from all over the world for the support of this pet project of mercy. She has led in the establishment of the co-operatives, the war work of China's women, the care of the wounded, the education of children, and the rehabilitation of the millions driven from their homes by the ruthless Japanese. The recent history of China has in large degree centered in this remarkable woman.

In the midst of the dangers and duties of the war the Chiangs have maintained their Christian activity. In bombed and blasted Chungking the Chiang home resembles the Soong home in Shanghai. In 1942 a Canadian friend spent an evening with the couple. The visitor looked at magazines while Madame Chiang was writing quietly at her desk. A servant approached, went away, and the writing continued. Soon she laid aside her pen and said, "In a few minutes there will be an aerial bombardment. Will you accompany me into the garden?" Then the Generalissimo arrived, the lights went out, and the planes came over, dropping bombs that destroyed an entire city block. Just as quietly Madame Chiang led them back into the house. After dinner the Generalissimo invited the guest to remain for family prayers. Chiang himself read a chapter from the Bible and prayed. Writes the visitor:

For the remainder of my life I do not expect to hear another prayer like that. The General began with a simple expression of gratitude for the courage of the nation under fire. He then prayed for strength and energy for the men in the fields of labor and for those who were in the firing line. He prayed that God would give him strength, and, in a special way, wisdom and direction, so that he might not abandon his people. But what impressed me most of all was his request that God would help China not to hate the Japanese people. He prayed for all Japanese Christians, and for the multitudes of Japan who were being impoverished to make the war in China possible. He prayed for the town that had been the victim of the bombardment, and also for those who were dropping the bombs. Then in a simple and humble way he placed himself afresh in God's hands, praying that he might know the Divine will so as to put it into practice on the morrow.

7

Mayling Soong Chiang Returns to America

ONE day in 1942 President Roosevelt announced that Madame Chiang Kai-shek had arrived in America for treatment in an unnamed hospital, and that she would be a guest at the White House when her physical condition permitted. It was said that she was suffering from the nervous strain of her almost superhuman war efforts and also from the result of an automobile accident several months before.

The name of the New York hospital in which she was resting was not published, but it became an open secret, and there was speculation on the exact nature of her trouble and rumors greatly exaggerating its seriousness. What really was back of her presence here? Had she come to demand greater American aid for China, or to confer with the President, as Mr. Churchill had done, on matters of military and postwar strategy? Her visit could not be for reasons of health alone, for she was accompanied by the Chinese vice-minister of information and a large entourage; she had taken an entire floor of one of the greatest hospitals and turned it into a little headquarters of Chinese officialdom! Much interest was aroused by the presence of this glamorous woman. She was not a private individual revisiting a country she loved in pursuit of health; she was an official personage of almost fabulous standing.

At a press conference in New York she later answered some of these questions. She had no official mission whatever, she declared, but came solely for health reasons; it was essential, for she was suffering, and there were no adequate modern facilities in Chungking—not even X-rays. But she had received two thousand letters and telegrams a day, from all parts of the country, all types of people, and all kinds of institutions and groups. She was swamped with invitations to visit and speak in cities, legislatures, colleges, clubs. Because of such evidences of kindness and good will, she continued, she felt it her duty to respond in some degree and represent China to the American people.

A sentimental reporter wanted to know how her husband was induced to agree and whether he was not greatly worried because of the danger involved. Madame Chiang replied simply that there was no question of agreeing or disagreeing, but only one of necessity, and that there was relief on all faces when she consented to undertake the journey.

Wendell Willkie has thrown a sidelight on the visit:

Just before we were to leave, Madame Chiang said to Dr. and Madame Kung: "Last night at dinner Mr. Willkie suggested that I should go to America on a good-will tour." The Kungs looked at me as if questioning. I said: "That is correct, and I know I am right in suggesting it."

Then Dr. Kung spoke, seriously. "Mr. Willkie, do you really mean that, and, if so, why?"

I said to him, "Dr. Kung, you know from our conversation how strongly I believe that it is vital for my fellow countrymen to understand the problems of Asia and the viewpoint of its people, how sure I am that the future peace of the world probably lies in a just solution of the problems of the Orient after the war.

"Someone from this section with brains and persuasiveness and moral force must help educate us about China and India and their people. Madame would be the perfect ambassador.

Her great ability—and I know she will excuse me for speaking so personally—her great devotion to China, are well known in the United States. She would find herself not only beloved, but immensely effective. We would listen to her as to no one else. With wit and charm, a generous and understanding heart, a gracious and beautiful manner and appearance, and a burning conviction, she is just what we need as a visitor." [1]

The story of her "invasion" of America and "taking the country by charm" is one of the beautiful epics of the war years. In modern times probably no woman has been so acclaimed; every appearance was an ovation, and no auditorium was large enough for her audience. No visitor to these shores in living memory made such an impression. America became "China-conscious" and the sympathy of the people for their great Oriental ally was newly cemented by her words and personality.

"Mme. Chiang a Hit Everywhere," screamed a headline in New York; and a "sob sister" thus described her first public appearance in the metropolis inured to dignitaries and noted figures of every sort:

The tremor of excitement that pulsed through the Monday routine of City Hall Park today broke to the surface when Mme. Chiang Kai-shek stepped up before the crowd and said: "Fellow citizens of New York. . . . ." Her audience hung on every one of the beautifully clear, softly sounded words that fell from her lips. Sometimes someone whispered under his breath, and it was always an expression of almost incoherent admiration. . . . .

Uptown, downtown, in subways, in cabs, on corners, in offices, in penthouses, in kitchens, the word was passed today in anticipation of her arrival. Girls going to downtown offices made

---

[1] *One World* (New York: Simon & Schuster, 1943), p. 58.

dates to spend their lunch hour in Chinatown. Shoppers bombarded policemen for information about what hour her car would pass. At the Waldorf-Astoria, where she is staying, cigarette girls, waiters, and porters crowded into doorways with the mink- and sable-clad residents of the Waldorf Towers to catch a glimpse of Mme. Chiang Kai-shek as she was whisked to and from her rooms. Waiters suddenly found that they must carry trays through the doorway at the time she was due to pass. . . . . "Pretty" was the first word that came to people's minds, but it was more than that which held them spellbound. It was the appealing dignity of Mme. Chiang, the sad, gentle set of her face, and its appreciation of her wisdom that made New York thrill before this representative of China's millions.

Madame Chiang clearly showed the strain of her illness, and on more than one public occasion she required the ministration of a physician or nurse to enable her to carry through her part of the function, but with surprising courage and fortitude she continued to show herself and speak to the people about her country. She wore elegant Chinese dresses, but in spite of her attire her presence recalled her earlier words, "The only thing Oriental about me is my face."

She spoke in faultless English with lingering traces of the soft accent of Georgia, and her vocabulary and knowledge of American history was marked. She sent the journalists scurrying to their dictionaries with some of her expressions, and they always found she had used the right word in the right place. She spoke of "the Gobineaus and the Houston Chamberlains" of Germany, and the "brawn and thews" of the American pioneers, and declared that at the peace table the United Nations "will not be obtunded by the mirage of contingent reasons of expediency." In a speech at Chicago she cited the opposing policies of Thomas Jefferson and Alexander Hamilton in the early history of the United States and said, "As I see it, the present American society is actually the very evolvement of a happy culmination of Hamilton's and Jefferson's ideals forged into one. The seemingly repellent opposites have produced an epochal synthesis, for the fundaments of supreme reason in man, for the most part, enjoin the must and forbid the contrary." She spoke of the torch of liberty shining with effulgence, rendering the world "perdurable for peace," the "warning voices which echoed small and still across the vast wilderness of indifference and nescience," and "the atonality of discord." Easily, naturally, without trace of pedantry, she caused Americans to blink at her use of their own language.

Leaving the hospital in New York, Madame Chiang went to Washington as the guest of President and Mrs. Roosevelt. It was her first public gesture in the country. She carefully refrained from making a direct appeal for more military aid for China, but soon important men in Congress were saying that increased assistance must be forthcoming. At a press conference in the executive offices President Roosevelt told the correspondents that America would send material to China "as fast as the Lord will let us." Madame Chiang smiling pointed out that "the Lord helps those who help themselves."

China's First Lady spoke to the United States Senate and the House of Representatives; she and Queen Wilhelmina of the Netherlands are the only women not members who have ever addressed the Congress. Her remarks in the Senate were entirely extemporaneous, prefaced by the statement, "I am not a very good extemporaneous speaker; in fact, I am no speaker at all." But she made a very effective informal speech, in which she commented: "The traditional friendship between your country and mine has a history of 160 years. I feel that there are a great many similarities between your people and mine, and that these similarities are the basis of our friendship."

She spoke of China's adherence to the four freedoms expounded by President Roosevelt and declared that the ideals must not "echo as empty phrases but become realities for ourselves, for our children, for our children's children, and for all mankind." She illustrated the necessity of active struggle for translating high hopes into actualities in the postwar world by a story:

One day we went into the Heng-Yang Mountains, where there are traces of a famous pavilion called "rub-the-mirror" pavilion. Two thousand years ago near that spot was an old Buddhist temple. One of the young monks sat cross-legged with his hands clasped before him in an attitude of prayer, and murmured, "Amita-Buddha! Amita-Buddha! Amita-Buddha!" He murmured and chanted day after day, because he hoped that he would acquire grace. The father prior of that temple took a piece of brick and rubbed it against a stone, hour after hour, day after day, and week after week. So one day the young acolyte said to him, "Father prior, what are you doing day after day rubbing this brick on the stone?" The father prior replied, "I am trying to make a mirror out of this brick." The young acolyte said, "But it is impossible to make a mirror out of a brick, father prior." "Yes," said the father prior, "it is just as impossible for you to acquire grace by doing nothing except murmur 'Amita-Buddha' all day long day in and day out."

Madame Chiang displayed unusual talent in citing historical illustrations to vivify her messages and clinch her meaning. In her outdoor address at the City Hall in New York she said:

If we thought that we were fighting alone, if we thought we were fighting only for China, to be very frank with you, China would not be the China of today, but would have been a conquered China. But we realized that justice will prevail, and that the people of America knew and realized what was at stake.

Perhaps I can best illustrate to you what I mean by a little story. More than two thousand years ago, in the reign of Tsin-Shi-Wang, the emperor who built the Great Wall, there were in the Province of Kwangsi two rivers which were continually overflowing, and causing death and destruction to many thousands of people in that part of the country. The emperor sent a very high official to build dykes to prevent floods. The official failed and he paid the final penalty for his failure. The emperor then sent a second official. The second official also failed. He too paid the final penalty. Finally he sent a third man. This man succeeded and high honors were bestowed upon him. When I visited the spot last year with the Generalissimo, we found three graves there. I asked, "Why are there three graves?" and I was told: "These are the graves of the three men, the two who had attempted to make the dyke and failed, and the third who succeeded." I asked why was the third man buried with the other two. And the reply was that when the third official succeeded and honors were bestowed upon him, he declined the honors and killed himself because, he said, he could not profit by the failure of others. In other words, he disdained to benefit himself by the price others had paid with their lives.

I feel that the American people have the same highmindedness. They would not benefit from the price anyone else has paid for liberty or freedom. This highmindedness, this integrity, this feeling that we shall suffer with others, and together work and strive for a common cause, constitute the common meeting ground for your people and mine.

In her Chicago address she said:

There are peoples and nations who are yet bent on tramping underfoot the inalienable rights and dignity of men. They have not the eyes to see that over the blue horizon, beyond the smoky ruins following in the wake of the bursting bombs, there is a vision of a new world—a world founded on practiced justice and equality for all mankind. The following anecdote may help us to understand the power of faith:

Right: MADAME CHIANG EN-
TERTAINS WENDELL WILLKIE
IN CHUNGKING
Later he suggested she visit
the United States

Below: MADAME CHIANG IN
MADISON SQUARE GARDEN
Left to right: Governor Dewey
of New York, Madame Chiang
John D. Rockefeller, Jr., Ma-
dame T. V. Soong, Willkie

Above: MADAME CHIANG VISITS THE PRESIDENT

Below: MADAME CHIANG ATTENDS CHURCH

With Vice-President and Mrs. Wallace at Foundry Methodist Church, Washington, D. C., the Rev. Frederick Brown Harris (*right*), pastor

When Confucius was on his way to return to the Kingdom of the Lu from the Kingdom of Wei, he and his party rested on the bank of a river. Below was a waterfall of several hundred feet. On the opposite bank a man started to swim across the river. Confucius sent a disciple to stop him, "Cannot you see that here is a waterfall of several hundred feet with miles of whirlpools beneath it where not even fish or turtles can live?" The man replied, "Do not mind me," and swam across. In astonishment Confucius asked him, "What skill or magic do you possess so that you can jump into this whirlpool and come out safe?" The man replied. "When I plunge into the river, I have faith in myself. When I swim in the current, I keep my faith in the water. My faith protects me in the current and I do not think about myself." Turning to his disciples, Confucius said, "If a man can swim across such a river through faith, what cannot be accomplished by having faith in man?"

To translate, however, faith into reality, you and I must recapture faith in our fellow men in the spirit of your pioneer fathers who forged in the van of the movement westward and forward in cutting across the wilderness and endless forests. We should march onward with staunch hearts and steadfast will in the cultivation of what William James calls tough-mindedness—tough-mindedness while searching for rectitude and truth in the triumph of a just and permanent peace. Let us then together resolve to keep on fighting in the faith that our vision is worth preserving, and can be preserved. For is it not true that faith is "the substance of things hoped for, the evidence of things not seen"?

In her Madison Square Garden address at New York City occurred this passage:

Tyranny and dictatorships have been proven to be short-lived. We ask ourselves why is it that the ancient Persian Empire only remained at its comparative zenith for a few centuries, while the high tide of the Napoleonic era only lasted for a few decades?

We read that Sapor, the Persian Emperor, after defeating the Romans, used the neck of Valerian, the Roman Emperor, as a footstool for mounting his horse. Was it this cruelty and arrogance of the conqueror toward the conquered which contributed to the fall of the dictatorships whose leaders strutted about in a frenzy of exhibitionism during their short day as invincible conquerors and masters?

Let us contrast this with the Chinese way of life as shown in the following historical incident: During the period of the Three Kingdoms in China, Kuan Kung, a valiant warrior, met Huang Tsung, also a brave warrior, in single combat. With a sweep of his long sword, Kuan Kung cut off the forelegs of his opponent's steed. Horse and rider both toppled to the ground. The vanquished warrior awaited his doom with resignation. The victor, Kuan Kung, however, extended his weaponless hand and cried: "Arise! My sword falls edgeless against a dismounted and unarmed foe."

Madame Chiang's speech before the House of Representatives struck the note of high idealism which characterized every utterance made by her to the American people.

The 160 years of traditional friendship between our two great peoples, China and America, which has never been marred by misunderstandings, is unsurpassed in the annals of the world. I can also assure you that China is eager and ready to co-operate with you and other peoples to lay a true and lasting foundation for a sane and progressive world society which would make it impossible for any arrogant or predatory neighbor to plung future generations into another orgy of blood.

In the past China has not computed the cost to her manpower in her fight against aggression, although she well realized that manpower is the real wealth of a nation and it takes generations to grow it. She has been soberly conscious of her responsibilities and has not concerned herself with privileges and gains which she might have obtained through compromise of principles. Nor will she demean herself and all she holds dear to the practices of the market place. We in China, like you, want a better world not for ourselves alone but for all mankind, and we must have it. It is not enough, however, to proclaim our ideals or even to be convinced that we have them. In order to preserve, uphold and maintain them, there are times when we should throw all we cherish into our effort to fulfill these ideals even at the risk of failure.

Madame Chiang said little in direct fashion about religion or her relation to the Christian world movement, but the nature of her messages in their entirety expressed her Christian attitude more effectively than a sermon, and the significance of this was not lost upon the nation. In New York City a monster reception was arranged in Madison Square Garden. Twenty thousand people attended. Among those who paid tribute to Madame Chiang and to China on the occasion were John D. Rockefeller, Jr.; Wendell Willkie; Mayor F. H. LaGuardia; Lieutenant General H. H. Arnold, chief of the United States Air Forces; Bishop Herbert Welch, of the Methodist Church; the most Rev. J. Francis A. McIntyre, Roman Catholic Auxiliary Bishop of New York; Dr. Henry Sloane Coffin, president of Union Theological Seminary; Lawrence Tibbett, of the Metropolitan Opera Company; Lieutenant Commander Mildred H. McAfee, commander of the WAVES and president of Wellesley College; Governor Thomas E. Dewey of New York; and the governors of the eight other North Atlantic states. The master of ceremonies in an energetic moment declared that "the Japs will be exterminated like all other termites." Madame Chiang said in her address:

All nations, great and small, must have equal opportunity of development. Those who are stronger and more advanced should consider their strength as a trust to be used to help the weaker nations to fit themselves for full self-government and not to exploit them. Exploitation is spiritually as degrading to the exploiter as to the exploited.

Then, too, there must be no bitterness in the reconstructed world. No matter what we have undergone and suffered, we must try to forgive those who injured us and remember only the lesson gained thereby.

The teachings of Christ radiate ideas for the elevation of souls and intellectual capacities far above the common passions of hate and degradation. He taught us to help our less fortunate fellow beings, to work and strive for their betterment without ever deceiving ourselves and others by pretending that tragedy and ugliness do not exist. He taught us to hate the evil in men, but not men themselves.

The effect of these words was electrical, not only in the vast and cheering audience but throughout the country. It was made the lead in the story of the event published in the New York papers the following morning:

Mme. Chiang Kai-shek, wife of fighting China's Generalissimo, asked the United Nations last night to repudiate thoughts of bitterness and revenge when the enemy has at last been defeated and the time has come to build a better world. The slender, charming woman whose homeland has been ravaged and bombed savagely for 2,064 straight days by the Japanese, spoke her simple Christian plea in Madison Square Garden before a distinguished audience of 20,000 persons which met to hear the first major public address of her New York visit.

The *New York Herald Tribune's* leading editorial the next day was headed "There Must Be No Bitterness."

Madame Chiang did not hesitate to voice her moral indignation against the acts of her nation's enemies and to repudiate the principles represented by them. Wendell Willkie, in presenting her to the New York audience, said, "She is an angel, but an avenging angel." She said the "most deeply dyed aggressors were inspired by unrighteous pride run absolutely mad," and declared that "the Axis powers have shown that they have no respect for anything but brute force and, such being the case, they logically hold that conquered peoples should become shackled slaves. . . . . We in China have bled for the last six long years to demonstrate our repudiation of [their] inert and humiliating philosophy."

Speaking to an immense throng in the Hollywood Bowl in California she told of her arrival in Soochow after the railway station had been bombed. Hundreds of wounded soldiers were streaming in, and as her party walked across the platform they waded through human blood, which soaked through their shoes and stockings and stained their feet. A wounded soldier tugged at her skirt and cried out for water. As she turned to answer his cry a physician told her the boy had a stomach wound and must not take water. Could she ever forget the look of agony on that boy's face when she told him that for his own sake she could not give him a cup of water! Her voice choked and stopped with emotion as she related the incident, and many in the audience wept.

But in all this Madame Chiang never uttered a low word, never descended to rabble rousing, never spoke except as became a Christian. A careful reading of her speeches fails to reveal a bitter word. Even the story of the tragedy at Soochow was coupled with the statement that the Chinese people had kept hate out of their hearts.

In New York and in California she visited and spoke to her own people. In New York:

Chinatown, scrubbed spotless and bedecked with flags and banners, turned out in almost silent homage as Mrs. Chiang Kai-shek, heroic, petite symbol of Chinese courage and fortitude, made a fleeting visit to the community of her former countrymen. To the thousands of Chinese who thronged the narrow, winding streets, the visit was too short. The most memorable occasion in the seven or eight decades of the quarter's history seemed to pass like a flash. Many thousands of Chinese from other parts of the city and from outlying areas joined Chinatown's 5,000 residents for the occasion. Police estimated that perhaps 50,000 Chinese and several hundred Caucasians lined Mott Street, with its Oriental facades and ancient buildings, when the entourage of the wife of generalissimo arrived.

In speaking to the Chinese, Madame Chiang urged them to have pride in their race and the history and achievements of China, but to avoid any form of pride that professed superiority or depreciated the worth and contributions of other peoples.

At her press conference in the Waldorf Astoria Hotel in New York, Madame Chiang, obviously under great nervous and physical strain, greeted a number of journalists and demonstrated the alertness of her mind and her sense of diplomacy by skillfully turning aside every inappropriate or "catch" question. Asked if she had invited Mrs. Roosevelt to visit China, she laughed merrily and invited the group present to visit her country. Would she return to China by way of England? The Japanese would be glad to know the route she would take! How did the Japanese women feel about the war? The Japanese women did not confide in her! A reporter with the air of a crusader said much consideration was being devoted to the occupied lands of Poland, Norway, Belgium, and Holland, but "what about the long-occupied lands of Africa and Asia?" Madame Chiang did not understand him and drew out the fact that he was trying to raise colonial questions. She replied that the wisest men of the world had not yet been able to solve these problems, and she was not very wise at all!

Madame Chiang was asked to comment upon the duty of the church in connection with the problems of the postwar world. She replied that in Washington she had been visited by all the bishops of the Methodist Church, and what she told them might be repeated. The function of religion, she said, was not only to save individual souls; it had a social mission as well. It is interested not solely in eternal life, but also in this present world. The church must seek to build the Kingdom of God here and now.

Wellesley College made Madame Chiang a member of Phi Beta Kappa when she visited the campus of her alma mater. Wesleyan College at Macon conferred the honorary degree of Doctor of Laws on her and also on Madame Kung and Madame Sun. Madame Chiang's last public act in America was to visit Wesleyan and her long-time friend and "other mother," Mrs. Ainsworth, widow of the former president of the college and bishop in charge of the China Mission.

While a guest at the White House in Washington, Madame Chiang attended religious services at the Foundry Methodist Church, sending an advance request that no notice be taken of her presence, since she desired only to worship God. She was accompanied by Vice President and Mrs. Wallace and several other official dignitaries. The chancel contained the flags of China and the United States and a basket of flowers with an inscription stating that they were given "in gratitude and admiration of two great servants of God and humanity whose lives are as candles of the Lord, Generalissimo and Madame Chiang Kai-shek." In the prayer of the pastor, Dr. Frederick Brown Harris, who is also chaplain of the United States Senate, were these words:

In the courts of Thy house we lift this day the starry emblem of our free land and the banner of our brave comrade in arms across the wide Pacific. As China's flag touches ours in this hallowed sanctuary, we are shamed by her sacrifice, inspired by her courage, humbled by her patience, and strengthened by her endurance as with the print of the nails she drinks the red cup in the garden of agony and waits with undimmed faith for emancipation and her rightful place in the Father's world. Steel our will to put into her waiting hands the weapons which will enable her to hurl the ruthless invader from her good earth and to plant there a garden of plenty and to build there the City of God. Make us worthy in the testing days to come to link our flag with hers as without vengeance or hatred we bear our banners together into a world made free for all men everywhere.

Bibliography

BOOKS

Burke, James: *My Father in China.* New York: Farrar & Rinehart, 1942.

Chiang Kai-shek, Generalissimo: *All We Are and All We Have* (addresses). New York: John Day Co., 1943.

————: *This Is Our China.* New York: Harper & Bros., 1940.

Chiang Kai-shek, Madame: *Sian, a Coup d'État.* Shanghai: China Publishing Co., 1937.

————: *We Chinese Women* (addresses). New York: John Day Co., 1943.

Hahn, Emily: *The Soong Sisters.* New York: Doubleday, Doran & Co., 1941.

Sheean, Vincent: *Personal History.* New York: Doubleday, Doran & Co., 1934.

Tong, Hollington K.: *Chiang Kai-shek: Soldier and Statesman.* 2 vols. Shanghai: China Publishing Co., 1937.

Willkie, Wendell L.: *One World.* New York: Simon & Schuster, 1943.

ARTICLES

Ainsworth, W. N.: "The Mountain Moves," *The Missionary Voice,* April, 1930.

Alsup, Alice: "China and the Revolution," *The Missionary Voice,* November, 1929.

Barnett, Fred T.: "The Romance of Charlie Soong," *The Duke Divinity School Bulletin,* January, 1942.

Chiang Kai-shek, Generalissimo: "I Have Been a Christian Now for Nearly Ten Years," *World Outlook,* July, 1937.

Chiang Kai-shek, Madame: "Missionaries in China Are Heroic," *World Outlook,* August, 1938.

————: "Religion and the Challenge to Civilization," *World Out-. look,* June, 1940.

————: "What Religion Means to Me," *Forum,* March, 1934, pp. 131-34.

Chiang Kai-shek, President and Mrs.: "Letter to American Christians," *World Outlook,* May, 1934.

Claiborne, Elizabeth: "Leaders of China Republic," *The Missionary Voice,* December, 1928.

————: "Mrs. K. T. Soong—Her Day," *The Missionary Voice,* December, 1931.

Eddy, Sherwood: "China's Christian General," *The Missionary Voice,* August, 1923.

Harrell, Costen J.: "General Carr and the Education of Charles J. Soong," *World Outlook,* September, 1943.

Hauser, Ernest O.: "China's Soong," *Life,* March 24, 1941.

Lew, T. T.: "Address at Dedication of the Charlie Jones Soong Memorial Building, Wilmington, N. C.," *North Carolina Christian Advocate,* May 6, 1943.

Moore, Louis T.: "Recollections of 'Charlie Soong,' " *World Outlook,* August, 1938.

Orr, John C.: "Recollections of Charlie Soon," *World Outlook,* April, 1938.

Quillian, Mrs. W. F.: "Intimate Glimpses of China," *World Outlook,* April, 1936.

Shepherd, George W.: "Close-up of General and Madame Chiang Kai-shek," *World Outlook,* March, 1938.

Sokolsky, George E.: "Troubled China Hears a Woman Speak," *The New York Times Magazine,* January 10, 1932.

Sun Yat-sen, Madame: "The Chinese Woman's Fight for Freedom," *Asia,* July, August, 1942.

"All Eyes on China," *The Missionary Voice,* April, 1927.

"Chinese Cabinet and the House of Soong, The," *The Missionary Voice,* January, 1929.

"I Feel the Need of a God Such as Jesus Christ," *The Missionary Voice,* December, 1930.

"Jehovah Will Do a New Thing, Make a Woman Protect a Man," *World Outlook,* July, 1937.

"Madame Chiang Kai-shek Greets General Conference," *World Outlook,* August, 1938.

"Personalities in the News," *The China Journal,* February, 1939.

"President of China Becomes a Christian, The," *The Missionary Voice,* December, 1930.

"T. V. Soong," *Current Biography,* 1941.